I0663964

OUR ALIEN HOURS

APOCALYPTIC TALES

ROBERT CHAZZ CHUTE

OUR ALIEN HOURS

Please direct media and rights inquiries to Holly at expartepress@gmail.com.

ISBN (Ebook) 978-1-927607-83-1
ISBN (Paperback) 978-1-927607-82-4
ISBN (Hardcover) 978-1-927607-83-1

PRAISE FOR ROBERT'S WORK

If you're tired of the formulaic schlock that clutters dystopian literature, then you need to read Endemic. The author has created a unique tale that serves up the best of deep characterization, nuanced plot, and emotional impact. Read this and you'll soon be looking for other books by Robert Chazz Chute. ~ From author RF Kacy's review of *Endemic.*

Robert Chazz Chute pulls no punches. Even in writing about a topic we're all presently living through, he easily ups the ante and makes his reader feel like we're all holding on for dear life. ~ phxazlaura, Amazon reviewer.

Robert Chazz Chute does not write escapist literature. He extrapolates the present into plausible but decidedly unwanted futures. ~ Russell Sawatsky, Amazon reviewer.

Chute sucks you in from word one and pulls you down his post-apocalyptic rabbit hole! You will sleep with the lights on, covers pulled over your head, and dust off the old teddy bear for comfort.

Chazz ranks among the top tier of our generation's storytellers. ~ Alex Kimmell, Author of *The Key to Everything*

Robert Chazz Chute is such a skilled spinner of tales that the reader is more than willing to suspend any possible disbelief to go along for the ride. ~ David Pandolfe, author of *Jump When Ready*

It's not very often one finds a writer with such a dark side that has such a great sense of humor. ~ Glenn Roberts, Amazon reviewer

The author has a definite talent with words and ideas. ~ Love to Read!, Amazon reviewer

His words lift and dance off the page, bringing the story to life. ~ Kindle Customer, Amazon reviewer

The world-building is horrifically well done with twists and turns and deceit around every corner. ~ Wanda, Amazon reviewer

RCC blends characters' beliefs & worries concerning society's failures, plus vivid action scenes skillfully. ~ RMerkl, Amazon Reviewer

Nothing but sheer exhaustion could tear my eyes from the captivating dance of words choreographed by Robert Chazz Chute. ~ Halph Staph, Amazon reviewer

Wonderful action constantly holds your interest. ~ Sharon Finn, Amazon reviewer

The complexity and attention to detail throughout absolutely blow me away. ~ Kindle customer, Amazon Reviewer

Very few authors impress me with their actual writing style, it's usually always about the story. But this author paints such beautiful vivid pictures with words that I found myself not only enjoying the story but enjoying the way the words created images in my mind. I know that sounds corny, but it is true. ~ B.H., Amazon reviewer

Chute gives us a story worthy of Stephen King. A read both thoughtful and fun. ~ Linda Beer Johnson, Amazon reviewer

The author does an excellent job building the characters and getting you invested and involved. ~ Michele L. Hebert, Amazon reviewer

I just can't say in words what a powerful author this is! ~ Delinda L. Calkins, Amazon reviewer

Robert Chazz Chute writes so skillfully as to make the supernatural seem perfectly logical and terrifying! There are twists, turns, and surprises galore. You will be glad you bought this book until you lose sleep because you can't put it down. ~ johligo, Amazon reviewer

When I want to read apocalyptic books or zombie stories, those books have to also be extremely well written and something that I could recommend with zeal and confidence to everyone I know. Robert Chazz Chute's books are exactly that. ~ Mazie Lane, Amazon reviewer

He makes the stuff that is obviously fiction, believable. ~ W. Nickels, Amazon reviewer

I am a lover of paranormal, dystopian novels and depth of story as well as intelligence in writing style, and Robert has it all. Humor, wit, depth, intelligence, and an awesome way with words/writing. ~ Amazon Customer, Amazon reviewer

For Russ,
because this is the one he's been waiting for.

For Alex,
because he couldn't wait.

INTRODUCTION

As I write this, I'm coming down from an hour of flirting with a panic attack. I should clarify: *another* panic attack. If you haven't had that experience, imagine drowning in a coffin. That probably comes close. The pandemic is troublesome, and I have been working in isolation for a long time.

I am continually frustrated and alarmed at the gap between how things are and how much better they could be. Chances are excellent that you share my frustration. I am compelled to write about that gap. Or should I call it the yawning chasm opening at our feet that's about to swallow us?

To escape science fact, I escape into science fiction. A long time ago, I read a story about explorers from Earth arriving on a dead planet. One brief description stuck with me. The narrator observed that the entire populace had perished by some inexorable cataclysm. The end had come swiftly and was so inescapable that families exited their front doors, stood together to look to the sky, and waited patiently to witness the end of the world.

That peaceful end was *not* Art imitating Life. It's clear now that people facing mass mortality could never be so equanimous. Recent events have illuminated much about human nature. Under stress, heroes and villains emerge. Others will stand awestruck, helpless, and bewildered at our collective folly.

In these seven linked stories, we'll explore what happens among humans when an irresistible force arrives on Earth. When faced with disaster, how do you suppose we will react? Many fight for the common good. Some only fight for themselves. Often, we do battle with ourselves. These are the kinds of struggles I play with in the *Apocalyptic Tales Series*. (If you like this one, try *Our Zombie Hours* and *All Empires Fall*, too.)

The experience you are about to have is as real as a dump truck bearing down on you. The brakes are shot, and the driver is drunk. Don't worry. We're safe here, so exploring the dark can still be fun. Turn the page, and let's see how — together and apart — we face disaster.

~ RCC
  January 2022
  Other London

I

There are two kinds of people:
me and everybody else.

~ The Solipsism Problem

TWO KINDS OF PEOPLE

As Evelyn Baxter touched up her lip gloss, the electricity died. Exasperated, she called out to her husband, "John? The power's out!" She picked up her phone to turn on her cellular data and check Twitter. "My phone's out of juice, too! Wouldn't you just know it? Can I use yours?"

John wandered into the bathroom behind her, feeling his way to avoid banging into anything. "My phone's dead, too. I was working in bed. Why don't we call it a night and come to bed? By morning, it'll be fixed."

She placed her lip gloss on the counter by the bathroom sink carefully. The apartment was so dark, she couldn't even make out his silhouette. "It's still early, though. What are we? Old? You know I wanted to get another video done tonight. I've got to tickle the algorithms. If I'm not putting myself out there, we stay trapped in here."

"If you're not on camera, you're dying. I get it." John ran his fingers through his hair and let out a long sigh. "Maybe this is a sign. When was the last time either of us went to bed at a decent hour?"

"That's the danger of two youngest children marrying each other, baby. No adults around to tell us when to go to bed."

"Is this about tickling the algos, or are you avoiding me?"

Taken aback, she said, "It's not all about you."

"Is anything?"

Evelyn couldn't see him, but she could hear his irritation. "Why would you say that?"

"Because I can't remember the last time you tickled me."

She pushed past him to their small living room. With the drapes to their one tiny window drawn, Evelyn couldn't see him any clearer than before. She found her way to the couch without stubbing a toe on the coffee table and sat down. "Do we have to go through this again? I know your policy: Don't go to bed mad. Stay up and fight!"

"I don't want to fight," he said.

"I want to make money. That's what this is about."

"And TikTok and Instagram is going to cover our nut? We're close to eviction, Evy. I think it's time we talked about polishing your resume again."

"Signing up for more shit jobs that pay shit isn't going to cover our monthly expenses."

"Either," John said. "You forgot to add the word *either*. Becoming a social media influencer — "

She corrected him, "*Being* a social media influencer."

"Okay, you had that one post that went viral — "

"It's a process, John. I told you that from the beginning. I warned you this would take time. Do you understand how quickly I can be forgotten if I don't keep pushing content? Every new video that isn't mine squishes my profile down."

"Honey, you do videos all day and night. You don't sleep — "

"This is a job. Advertisers hit me up in my DMs every day. Potential sponsors — "

"Scammers," John said flatly. "What about going back to the coffee shop? You got so much good material from that."

"From dealing with nasty customers, you mean. I want to do something different. I want to entertain and inform people. Slinging coffee? I felt trapped there. Might as well put my soul in the bean grinder. That's a good line. If my phone worked, I'd write that down."

"It's not that good," he muttered.

"What did you say?"

"Nothing."

She tapped her foot on the coffee table impatiently. "You know, maybe this is good. With the power out, we can't see each other's faces. It's easier to hash this out in the dark, you know? Maybe be more honest. Can you do that?"

"Talking into a void? That's what our life feels like lately. I'm putting in longer hours at work. You aren't sleeping because you're either doing TikTok or watching it. I'm not sleeping because I'm worried about the rent."

"This is America," Evelyn replied.

"I thought you wanted to be honest. You're quoting yourself."

"So?"

"I don't want recycled Evy. I want *my* Evy."

"I'm an artist."

"And I work for a living."

"You promised you'd be supportive."

John took a deep breath and let it out slowly. "When I say I work for a living, I mean I'm working for *you*."

"We've got to get out of this city," she replied.

"Not this again. My family is here."

"Way out on Staten Island, sure."

"So?"

"On the rare occasions we do see them, they amp you up about how much money we don't make and how crappy our basement apartment is. I honestly think your mom is where most of your stress comes from. The trouble doesn't come from what we don't have. You're angry because of your expectations of what you think we should have, what we should be."

Unable to see his wife's tears, he was emboldened. "I don't want to be homeless. This is math. Making the rent is tied to what we do, not what we think ought to be."

Jittery with nervous energy, John yearned to move around. Normally their one-bedroom apartment felt as tight as a coffin, but their argument made the short distance between them an uncrossable chasm.

Evelyn thought he would apologize and assure her he understood. John thought she wanted him to shut up. Each wanted the other to make them feel safe. Neither really hoped things would get better, but the comfort of being told it would all be okay was the one meager goal they both still shared.

The silence was broken by a far-off noise that made them both straighten and strain to hear more.

"What was that, do you think?" he asked.

"An explosion?"

"Couldn't be," he said. "Could it? I haven't heard one before. Have you?"

"Well? What do you think it was?"

"An explosion," John admitted.

"See? That's how we'll make progress. Seeing things for what they are."

To John, that sounded like a threat.

Evelyn rose quickly only to bang the little toe of her right foot on the leg of the couch. Stifling a curse, she reached up to part the drapes on their small window.

They saw what they always saw from their living room: a view of people's shoes passing by. However, the light was surprisingly dim, and people seemed to be in more of a hurry than usual, even for New York.

"Looks like the power's out everywhere," he said. "Haven't had a blackout in a long time."

"Yeah, but even our phones? I was sure I had at least a fifty percent charge."

Another explosion sounded somewhere in the distance.

"John? Let's find our shoes and get out there. Whatever's going on could be good content."

She was already making her way to the front door as John protested, "But our phones don't even work!"

"We'll take them. When the power comes back, I can go live. Even if they don't pop back on, whatever's happening, I can say I was there."

John scooped up his backpack by the front door and headed to their refrigerator. He grabbed a couple of water bottles and felt his way through a cupboard. In a moment, his hand closed on a box of energy bars. He stuffed that in the pack, too.

Evelyn snapped her fingers. "C'mon, Johnny. History's happening. If we see some, we make some!"

She stood halfway up the stairs to the street as he pulled on his shoes. As he fumbled with his keys to lock their apartment door, he warned, "I have to be at the restaurant early to do prep, Evy! Whatever's going on, at midnight I turn into a pumpkin."

"Don't worry about that. It's not even ten."

As they emerged at street level, the number of people on the street surprised them. A large man almost knocked John down as he rushed past.

Standing close to the door to their building, Evelyn complained, "If it weren't a full moon, I wouldn't be able to see your face. I wouldn't be able to see my hand in front of my face. No headlights, no phones — "

"This isn't like other blackouts," John said.

"How so?"

"The cars." He pointed at the vehicles, dead in the street.

"It's nuclear Armageddon," a man's voice declared.

They turned to find an old man they'd often seen at the mouth of the narrow alley next to their building. Ken Kim was a fixture of the neighborhood. He asked for money from passersby, and whether they gave him anything or not, he always called after them, "God bless!"

John sometimes brought home day-old pastries from the cafe where he worked and shared some of the leftovers with him. "Ken?" he asked. "You okay?"

"Ken Kim! That's me! I'm fine. It's the world that's messed up. That's the way it always was, but soon everyone will understand. I was never the crazy one, but in the Land of the Blind, the one who isn't listening to the news knows what's true!"

With some effort, the houseless man got to his feet and hobbled closer, leaning on his cane. "They've finally done it, huh? By accident, by hook, or by crook, they've finally done it! They blew it all up! Damn dirty apes! That's what we are, playing with weapons beyond our ken. I know because I'm Ken, and their nastiness is all beyond me!"

"What have you heard?" Evelyn asked.

"Oh, it's not what I've heard. Pay no attention to what you've heard. It's what you see. I was trained for this."

"Trained?" John pressed. "Trained for what?"

"Infantry, when I was younger than you. When some lights go out, some poor tired electrician dropped a wrench and got fried at a power station. But when they all go out? That's nuclear. Gotta be an EMP — electromagnetic pulse — and a big one. Whoever they are, they've taken out the greatest city in the world. We've always been a fat target, so nobody should be surprised. Russians, you think? That's all we worried about in my day, but it could be anybody now, couldn't it?"

"We need more information before we jump to conclusions," Evelyn suggested.

"I didn't jump to conclusions. Can't jump. I got a bum knee and an old cane the VA gave me. I step very carefully to my conclusions."

"Sorry, Mr. Kim. I meant no offense."

"None taken, of course, young lady. I sleep out here year-round, so there isn't anyone or anything that can hurt my feelings."

The old man gestured to the people hurrying past. There were too many for the narrow sidewalk so they walked down the middle of the street. "Look at all those people with their fancy stuff. *Heh*. They got beds and couches, so they're still ahead, I guess. Otherwise, they're no better off."

John and Evelyn took a moment to watch the dark silhouettes of people streaming by. It seemed like all of New York had received an unspoken message to pour out into the streets.

"Can you sense it?" Evelyn asked. "The excitement?"

"Excitement may be how it starts," Ken said, "but it zips up to fear and anger PDQ. Even by a little glow of moonlight, you can feel it in the way they move. People are worried. They're in a rush, even though they don't know where they're going."

"We're all always worried," John muttered.

"This is America," Evelyn whispered.

"Evy, please don't," John warned.

"They're not used to being this scared," Ken added. "You two should go home, if you don't mind me saying. Go to bed, cuddle up, and be glad you have each other. Scared people do silly things. Could get ugly out here."

"But ugly is where the adventure is," Evelyn replied.

"Nah, take it from Ken Kim! But ugly is just butt ugly."

As the couple walked away, he called after them, "God bless! God bless us all. We're gonna need it!"

They followed the crowd. Everyone seemed to be heading in the same direction. When they asked others in the crowd where they were headed, most said they were just caught up in the stream, following others.

"We're headed toward the sound of the explosions," someone explained.

"But what's going on?" Evelyn asked.

No one knew. The darkness was so all-consuming, they feared stopping lest they be trampled. A few younger people with glow sticks peppered the crowd, but the sticks offered little light. Several blocks on, John pulled Evelyn by her sleeve toward the edge of the river of humanity.

"I've got claustrophobia, Evy. I need a break. It's too dark and too many people."

As they came to a basketball court, they exited the street and stood in the middle of the court. John closed his eyes to slow his breathing. Behind them, at the rear of the court, a figure sat on the ground weeping.

"Hello?" Evelyn called. "Are you okay?"

They made their way toward the silhouette of the crying woman sitting under a basketball net. She was middle-aged, surrounded by shopping bags. A man lay beside her on his back. As she turned her face up to them, the moonlight made the tears on her cheeks glisten.

"This is my husband," the woman said. "Gary and I went out for dinner. It's our anniversary. We've had twenty-seven of them. This morning, I never imagined this would be the last."

Evelyn knelt and checked for a pulse at the man's wrist, then to be sure, checked again for a pulse at his neck. His body was still warm, but she was sure the man was dead. She'd seen documentaries, but she'd never seen a corpse up close before. She'd never even attended a funeral.

"I'm sure it was his heart," the woman explained. "He was fine earlier. He did everything right, but ..."

"Did he have a pacemaker?" John asked gently.

"How did you know?"

"Everything electrical is dead — er, not working."

The woman nodded. "I tried calling 911, but whatever's happened killed my phone just like it killed Gary. Can't even use the flashlight. Do you know what's going on? I know it's too late for an ambulance, but I don't know what to do. I can't just leave him here."

"Do you live in the neighborhood?" Evelyn probed. "Are you far from home?"

"Not far, but what should I *do*?"

John and Evelyn had no suggestions.

"I do have a landline at home," the woman ventured. "Do you suppose that might work? I could call the funeral home. Our family has one, but I thought we wouldn't have to worry about that for many —" She began to sob harder. "What am I going to do?"

Evelyn slipped an arm around the woman's shoulders. For several minutes, they simply sat together. The young couple wanted to offer words of condolence and encouragement, but helplessness silenced them. Words suddenly seemed small and feeble things, inadequate to combat the enormity of the woman's loss.

After some time, the widow straightened and wiped her tears.

"You two go on. I'm going to stay with Gary for a while, tell him things I forgot to say. Mostly I-love-yous." She let out a rueful laugh. "It seems I have the opportunity to have the last word, so maybe I'll settle a few petty arguments. We bickered quite a bit, but we never meant any of it...most of it."

Evelyn and John looked at each other. They argued a lot, and they were always deadly serious. Winning arguments suddenly seemed less important.

"Really, go on. I'll wait with him."

John cleared his throat. "Wait for what?"

The widow shrugged. "Dawn. For the power to come back on. For the end of the world. All the same to me."

They offered to walk her back to her apartment. The woman insisted she wanted to be left alone. She refused to leave the body, so they muttered their condolences and walked on.

"I feel guilty leaving her there like that," John admitted.

"There wasn't anything else we could do," Evelyn replied. "It's ... I don't know."

"Sad and frustrating to feel helpless?"

She shook her head. "I was going to say freeing. Seems like we have to make a thousand decisions a day. That woman is helpless because there's nothing more she can do. Nothing we can do. It's nice to have fewer choices to make."

John said nothing and his wife took his silence for agreement.

A few blocks farther, the couple came upon looters attempting to break into a hardware store. Two young men, one short, one tall, took turns using a long crowbar to pry apart the bars shielding a glass door.

One of the men looked over at them and nodded. "Give us a couple more minutes and we'll be in."

Evelyn pulled her husband's sleeve, urging him on, but John held back. "Only a few people seem to have working flashlights."

"We're too used to using our phones when we need one," the short one muttered. "Hell, I couldn't even pop my trunk."

"I got an old Chrysler LeBaron," the tall one added. "Keys still work in locks. I could get the crowbar out of my trunk, but my gun safe is electronic so it's fried. I couldn't find my keys to the gun safe in the dark, so here we are."

"What are you guys shopping for?" Evelyn asked.

The tall one strained at the bars, pulling on the crowbar with all his might. "Flashlights, batteries, whatever looks useful. Who knows how long this will last?"

The short man laughed. "I'm breaking my diet. Dibs on first pick of the chocolate bars by the front counter!"

Uneasy, Evelyn whispered to her husband, "We should get out of here, right?"

"We could use a light. We heard *explosions*, Evy. In a disaster, it's not looting. It's scavenging for survival. What if a building collapsed or something? Being able to see better would be a good start."

"I know that's right, but it feels wrong."

"Remember when my dad got sick?" John asked. "One day he was fine and that night he noticed the lump?"

"Jesus! Why are you bringing that up now?"

"When I took him to his first specialist's appointment, he couldn't get over how fast things can change."

"Oh," Evelyn said. "How fast they can turn bad, you mean."

John pulled his wife into a tight embrace and whispered in her ear, "That's what this is. We're going from normal to scary over the course of what? How long has it been? Twenty-five minutes? Forty? I've got whiplash, too, but we've got to adapt to changing circumstances, right?"

"Okay," Evelyn said. "We get a couple of flashlights, and then we get going as fast as we can. I feel like I'm missing a birth or something."

John joined the men to pull hard on the long lever. The bars did not move, but the gate broke away from its track enough for Evelyn to roll beneath it.

"Didn't use long enough screws on the frame," the tall man observed. "I work construction. When all this is over, I'll come back to help them get it right."

Evelyn stood with her back pressed to the door. "Don't let go of that thing or it'll break my face." She kicked backward with her heel.

"No, no, no!" the short man warned. "You either won't break through that way or, if you do, you'll open an artery. Use this." He produced a hammer from beneath his jacket.

It took several whacks to crack the glass and a lot more to clear the bottom panel of any shards.

"No alarm," John said. "I didn't really expect any, but I kind of expected it, too, if you know what I mean."

While John and the tall man held the gate back, Evelyn entered safely. The short man followed her inside. They might have rummaged through the dark store for hours if they had to make their way by feel. However, the short man had a book of matches, and little by little, they searched for something strong enough to prop the gate open.

Evelyn found the sledgehammers and grabbed two to use as a wedge. With great effort and a lot of sweat, the four managed to set the hammerheads against the iron bars and the handles against the base of the wall. When they were done, the hammers stood at a forty-five degree angle, propping the gate out from the entrance.

John and the tall man crawled beneath the gate, and still panting, entered the hardware store.

"I'm Todd," the tall man said and shook hands with John and Evelyn. "Thanks for the help. Working together is how we're going to get through whatever this is. Short stack over there gorging on candy is Avery." Todd called over to his companion, "Avery? If you get fat, I'll still love you, but I'll be mad about it."

"A man needs energy to do combat in the apocalypse." They could hear him peeling the wrapper from another candy bar.

Evelyn found boxes of matches by the cash register and handed them out. "First priority has to be batteries and flashlights. After that, we can find whatever else we need easily."

"Smart call," Todd agreed. "Avery, come help. The M&Ms are still gonna be there after we get some light in here!"

At that moment, a man's voice called from the front of the store,

"Hey! Is this where the party's at?" A young man and two women stood outside, waving in the moonlight.

"It's shopping time!" one of the women crowed.

The other young woman giggled. "Major discounts, tonight only!"

Todd rushed to the front of the store and put bass in his voice. "This is *our* store! You come in here, I'll shoot you! You got it? This is *ours*!"

The trio scurried away and only began to shout curses when they thought they were at a safe distance.

"Damn tourists," Todd said. "This isn't recreational. We aren't thieves. We're survivalists and we worked for it. Those wastoids will be smashing into a jewelry store next. Or trying to get high behind the counter of a CVS."

To everyone's relief, they found the batteries and flashlights. Fresh batteries worked and they were soon bathed in the glow of four flashlights.

"I know it's basic," Avery said, "but turning a light on has never felt so reassuring."

John found the rear exit. To deter interlopers, they pulled the sledgehammers, and the gate crashed back in place. They continued to search the store for useful supplies and were disappointed.

"This place is such a *city* hardware store," Avery complained. "I'm not looking to build a deck or hang a painting! I grew up in Wisconsin. You go into a hardware store in Wisconsin, you got everything from clothing and tractors to fertilizer for bombs."

Evelyn handed her husband a hammer and took one for herself.

"What the shit, Evy?"

"Defensive weapons," she said, "just in case."

"Just in case of what?"

"That's the point. We don't know yet."

Todd and Avery grinned as they armed themselves with gas powered nail guns.

"Nobody's going to mess with us now," Todd said.

As John stuffed candy, candles, and a couple of boxes of matches in his backpack, Evelyn asked, "What do you guys think is really going on?"

Todd answered without hesitation, "Cyberattack. Rachel Maddow warned us about hackers shutting down our power grid long ago."

Evelyn shook her head. "Even our phones?"

"Cyberattack, so especially our phones."

"And the cars?"

"Hackers can take over a car, so they took over all of them."

"*All* our electronic devices, though?" John shook his head. "Is your gun safe hooked up to the internet?"

Todd's shoulders sank. "Oh. Uh ... shit. I think maybe I need a new theory."

Avery looked surprised. "You've been talking about Russians blowing up our nuclear plants ever since those reports came out. I hate to say I told you so — "

"You love to say that."

Avery bobbed his head. "In emergency situations, it's good to find the glee."

John discovered a small office at the back of the store by the exit. A sawed-off shotgun sat atop a filing cabinet. He found a full box of cartridges in the bottom desk drawer. He slipped the weapon and ammunition into his backpack. John did not share news of his discovery with the others.

Avery walked in on John and almost caught him hiding the shotgun. Avery held up a radio in triumph. "Look what I found! Police scanner! Want to find out what's really going on? This is how."

John looked at the man skeptically. "You know all electronics are fried and nothing works and there's no hope, right? We passed a guy when we were out there. His wife had a good heart, he had a bad heart. The guy's pacemaker was a useless piece of shit."

"Like the flashlights," Avery said. "Add fresh batteries and maybe it will work."

Avery was right. Once they added three fresh D batteries from the rack, the scanner came to life. Zipping up and down the frequencies, they heard no fire department or police chatter, just a lot of static.

Evelyn was just about to tell John they should go when a harried woman's voice broke through the radio's whine and static. The woman did not identify herself, only mentioning that she was in the control tower at JFK International Airport.

Her voice quavering, she called for help that wasn't coming, "CQ! CQ! Two passenger jets are burning on the tarmac! There are more downrange, and none are in the air. We are obviously under attack. Our on-site first responders are overwhelmed. Please send help! We need fire and medical! Can anyone hear me?"

"She's frazzled," Evelyn said.

"Unless I go out on the gallery deck and scream, this is the only way I can call for help. Our backup systems have failed!"

John, Evelyn, Todd, and Avery stood transfixed.

"Sounds like something out of a movie," Evelyn observed.

"But it isn't!" John exclaimed. "This isn't a damn movie, Evy!"

"You don't think I know that?"

Todd cleared his throat. "Whoever she is, she doesn't really know much more than we do. She has no idea we're all in the same boat."

"And we're sinking," John said.

"This radio is only a receiver," Avery said. "We can't even tell her we're dead in the water."

As if to answer their frustrations, a man's voice came on the scanner to answer the woman at the airport. The signal was weak, and the voice was faint. "JFK? This is Kent Schreiber in Knock Station, Oregon. Do you read me? Over."

The woman replied sharply, "Clear this frequency, please. You can't help me from there, sir!"

Kent Schreiber's reply was chilling. "No help is coming, JFK. You're on your own. We all are."

Indignant, the woman came back harder, "You are not following proper radio protocol! What the hell are you saying?"

"JFK, the power outage is *global*. I've been in touch with a few hams in China, Indonesia, and Canada so far. The power is out everywhere. It's not just you. It gets worse. My friend in Bengkulu informs me the power outage was a prelude to invasion. A large ship emerged from the water, out of the Indian Ocean. Flew right overhead and didn't make a sound. Over."

"Mr. ... Schreiber, was it? I'll have your license pulled for this. Get off the air. I don't have time for trolls during a terrorist attack!"

Through the static, the ham radio operator's rueful laugh came through. "Good luck with that. Believe me or not, this is an invasion, JFK. Prepper networks are on alert for further sightings. These craft, whatever they are, are huge. Did you spot anything on radar before the power went out?"

There was a long pause before she answered, "Yes. But what we saw must have been an equipment malfunction. I'm signing off. This is pointless. I'm going down to the tarmac to see how I can help. If you have it in your heart, send help."

"All we've got for you is prayers, JFK. Good luck."

The radio fell silent. John shut off the scanner. When he looked up, Todd, Avery, and Evelyn looked back gravely.

"Who's gonna say it?" Todd asked. "I'm not."

"Me, neither," Avery said.

"Aliens," Evelyn said. "It's aliens."

"Well ... " Todd said finally, "I've got a nail gun."

"Maybe they'll want you to build them a deck," Avery suggested.

"What are we going to do?" John asked.

"If you've had enough candy," Todd told Avery, "we're going home. I found a battery-operated lantern for the bathroom. I only came out here because I wanted to make sure the toilet paper was clean when I was done wiping my ass."

Avery nodded sagely. "They can take our freedom, but at least the toilets still work. At least, I think they do. You guys want to come over? We've got a scrabble board and a lot of wine."

Evelyn shook her head. "Thanks, but I still want to witness history."

The short man put a hand on her shoulder and shook his head sadly. "This isn't *The Day The Earth Stood Still*."

"Meaning?"

"Look around. They aren't here on a mission of peace. You go looking for them, you'll witness the end of history. *We're* history."

"All the more reason to see the end," she replied.

"They say there are two kinds of people in the world," Todd said. "I don't know what they are, but I get the feeling we're not of the same kind. I can't wait to go home, drink Cabernet Sauvignon until I'm blind, and pull the covers over my head. Tell me all the news about the end of the world when it's over, and we're all in the afterlife."

Avery grinned. "Yup! That's why we're so good together. Total simpatico! When the going gets hopeless, the smart get drunk."

They used the rear exit and said their goodbyes at the front of the store. "I'd say see you around," Todd said, "but ... well."

Evelyn and John rejoined the moonlit parade of people heading south. The street was not as packed with people. The crowd had spread out and thinned. Evelyn set a fast pace. "I hope we aren't missing anything. Maybe we took too long in there."

John looked askance at his wife. "We aren't totally simpatico, are we?"

"What do you mean?"

He shrugged. "I'm not in the rush you are. What are we doing out here, Evy? Mr. Kim basically told us to go back to bed. We didn't even discuss it. We saw a woman mourning her dead husband, and the dead guy was right in front of us! Still, we didn't turn around and go home. Why do you have this burning need to see what's going on? We don't even know where we're going!"

"We're headed where everyone else is going."

"In the direction of the explosions, you mean. Please, stop to think about this. Give it a minute, and you'll see how crazy that sounds."

Evelyn pulled him aside, and they stopped on the sidewalk. She grabbed his shoulders, then pulled him into a hug, and held him tight to speak to him. "John, what makes us extraordinary?"

"What do you mean?"

"Let me put it another way. Where were you on 9/11?"

"In high school. They sent us home."

"But what did you do that day?"

"What everyone else did. We watched it on TV until we were sick of it."

"Todd was right. There are two kinds of people. I want to be the kind that does things and sees things."

"Even if it kills you?"

"If Avery and Todd are right, if that guy on the radio is right, we're all dead. I want to see it coming. I want to see as much of the future as I can. Aren't you curious?"

"Remember what curiosity did to the cat?"

"This isn't about how many likes and followers I get on Instagram anymore," she said. "If this is Earth's final chapter, I want to read to the end. Anybody could wait at home. Nobodies will wait at home. Going out to see them? People from another planet? You're talking danger and I'm talking adventure. Which kind of person are you?"

"I'm the third kind," John replied. "I don't care if I see aliens, and I do want to go home — "

"But?"

"But wherever you are is where I want to be."

She kissed him a long time. When they parted, Evelyn smiled. "Our fate, sealed with a kiss."

"I wish you hadn't said that part."

They followed the crowd for several more blocks until they got their first look at the alien craft hovering above the city. The spaceship had been nearly invisible, nothing more than a dark shape that reflected no moonlight. However, as bright red and green lights popped on, the jagged belly of the ship became clear.

Awestruck, Evelyn and John stood still for a moment, craning their necks skyward to take in the enormity of the ship.

"It's not what I expected," Evelyn whispered.

"What did you expect? A flying saucer?"

"Why not?" She shook her head, unable to look away. "I don't know. We can't see the top of it from here, but the underbelly looks like ... I'm not sure."

"Like an upside-down city," John suggested. "Like skyscrapers, but ground scrapers. Okay, you've seen an alien ship. What now?"

"We get closer. I have to see this thing."

Still looking up, the couple hurried to join the masses of New Yorkers gathered beneath it. They soon found themselves in Central Park.

The milling crowds were no longer silent. Excited whispers slipped through the mob. Some shouted in fear while others cheered in anticipation. Rounds of applause rose and died as everyone waited for something to happen, but no one knew what.

"These people obviously don't know about the planes burning at JFK," John said.

Evelyn shushed him. "You'll start a riot."

"Shouldn't we warn somebody?"

She looked around the crowd illuminated by the bright red and green strobe lights. "Nobody's leaving the park. Not now."

He wanted to jump up on a nearby rock and shout to the crowd, "This isn't an arrival! This is a hostile invasion! People have died!"

Sensing his nervous energy, Evelyn grabbed her husband's hand and told him to be quiet and watch.

After a few minutes, Evelyn nudged John in the ribs. "You ever notice that in the movies, aliens hate national monuments? They're always blowing up the White House and destroying the Eiffel Tower, that sort of thing."

"Blowing up the White House serves up a fantasy for a lot of people," John replied. "Pumps up the foreign box office."

"And the Eiffel Tower? How do you explain that?"

"They make a show of blowing up the Eiffel Tower so you know it's France. What else do we know about France? Blowing up a winery or a croissant factory isn't going to light us up. In the movies, no matter where you live in Paris, every apartment has a view of the Eiffel Tower. It's a trope, like every kid in America gets waffles for breakfast before school but rushes off with no time to eat them."

"Sure, sure, but why hover over Central Park?"

"Why not? We're in one of the largest cities in the world. If you look at New York from the air, the park stands out as a big rectangle. Looks like a logical landing zone for a spacecraft."

Evelyn shook her head. "That thing is too big to land."

"Maybe they'll beam down, like in *Star Trek*."

"And say, 'Take me to your leader?' Who's that going to be? I mean, is the mayor here? Are the aliens Democrats or Republican? What's the president's stance on these kinds of undocumented immigrants?"

As the alien craft hovered silently, the crowd became more restless and eager for something to happen. Children sat atop their parents' shoulders to get a better look. As the tension built, a few people stood on rocks and benches, rallying the assembled to join their chants.

The first was: Aliens! Come! On! Down!

When that died down, another rallying cry was simply, "Save us! Save us! Save us!"

An old man yelled through a rolled-up magazine. His voice held more dread. "It's the end times! Repent! Repent! The interdimensional demons are here to murder you and your children!"

John doubted the part about these intruders being demons from another dimension. However, he wanted to add his voice to the warning their intentions were malicious. However, Evelyn squeezed his hand so hard it almost hurt. It seemed only the entourage the old man brought with him were enthused by his message. The rest of the crowd booed and drowned him out.

Eventually, the old man stepped down from his park bench, giving up on saving the mob. "Enjoy Hell, Babylon!"

At that, laughter rippled through the crowd.

Weary of waiting, Evelyn pulled John over to a high rock overlooking the ice rink. There they waited, drinking the water they'd brought and munching on energy bars.

The flashing and spinning lights from the alien craft suddenly went dark. The crowd fell into silent shock. Then the lights brightened in long pulses, bathing Central Park in a light so bright, it was as well lit as noon on a sunny summer day. People shaded their eyes as they tried to keep their gaze fixed on the gigantic spacecraft.

"It feels like the anticipation I felt on Christmas morning when I was a kid!" Evelyn enthused. "You know that moment when you're maybe twelve or so? There are a bunch of presents under the tree for you. Somehow, in the back of your mind, you're a kid, but you *know* every Christmas after this one won't be quite as good. The presents are mostly for you, but next year you'll be a teenager. You'll be a little older, and there will be more little kids in the family. More little kids mean less for you, but this Christmas? This Christmas is mostly for and about you! You know that feeling, John?"

"I, uh, I can't say as I do."

"That's how it was for me. When's the last time you felt this kind of anticipation? I haven't felt this way since that last Christmas when it was all about me!"

"I've had that feeling plenty of times," John said. "The moment before I asked you on our first date was one. The night of our first date I wondered if you'd kiss me goodnight. The first night I knew we'd make love. The night before we got married. The day we got married — "

Evelyn did not look away from the spectacle above them, but she squeezed his hand gently. "You're sweet. Look! Someone must have broken into a candle store!"

Across the park, candles were being distributed. Slowly, the glow of hundreds of little flames spread from one candle bearer to the next.

Like a vigil, John thought uncomfortably.

Someone began to chant, "Om." The chant spread as more and more New Yorkers joined in. Some talented singers contributed harmonies and took off on tangents of arias before returning to the group's Om. It seemed every human voice was raised in a united show of welcome and solidarity with the visitors who had traveled so far to come to Earth.

The chanting faltered for only a moment as something detached from the craft. The crowd's energy surged as something lowered slowly to the ground. Without a word, the crowd backed away, making room.

Nearby, one woman's high voice cut through all other mutterings, "A gift from the space gods!"

People laughed, cheered, and applauded.

Standing on tiptoe, Evelyn asked, "What do you suppose it is? Can you see?"

John, who stood higher on the rock, reached down to pull her up beside him. He slipped behind her and wrapped her in a warm embrace.

A man yelled, "It looks like a big bathysphere! I bet they aren't used to the pressure of our gravity!"

That idea seemed to grip everyone's imagination, and most went silent and still.

Caught up in the moment, Evelyn yelled out for all to hear, "This is it! First contact!"

Someone hummed the five familiar notes from the movie *Close Encounters of the Third Kind.*

A new chant caught on. "Welcome to New York! Welcome to New York!"

John squeezed his wife tighter. "Whatever it is, it's history, this is what you wanted and we're seeing it!"

"Thank you, John! Thank you for giving me this, for being here with me."

John nuzzled her neck. "Don't thank me. I go where you go."

She patted his hand. "I'm just so happy you're here with me. What if you'd decided to stay home and pull the covers over your head?"

"You mean ... Evy?"

The thing that looked like a bathysphere settled on the ground just in front of the skating rink. The cable that lowered it detached and retracted. Though the machine was only about the size of a cube van, it must have been very heavy. It sank into the soil several feet.

"Evy!"

"What?"

Someone tried to start up the Om again, but the crowd went quiet, transfixed by the alien machine.

John whispered urgently, "If I hadn't gone with you, are you saying you would have gone without me?" His tight grip loosened.

From high above them, words never before spoken echoed across Central Park and across the city. The message from the alien ship was, "*Chumegan Kintela. Kintela Chumegan!*"

Many who heard it looked to others to repeat the alien words. Some spoke the unknown words with reverence. Others giggled at the idea they were mimicking words spoken by an unknown race from the stars.

"What do you suppose that means?" Evelyn asked.

"Could be anything," John replied. "'Greetings, puny humans,' would be my first guess. Or it could be, my C student got your A student pregnant."

She laughed and slapped his leg. "That's why we're together, baby. You make me laugh."

"That's it? That's all?"

Evelyn gave a tolerant smile, shrugged, and continued to ogle the mysterious vehicle.

Without a sound, the spacecraft began to gain altitude. Everyone looked up to follow the craft's trajectory.

One man's voice carried above all the others, "The mother ship! The mother ship is leaving!"

The round device that had settled into the ground began to spin on its central axis. Slowly, it rose. The machine crackled with electricity and began to spin faster.

Fresh doubt entered the minds of everyone in the crowd. John had a doubt of his own. "Evelyn? Tell me the truth! You really would have come here without me?"

She shrugged and pointed to the device the mother ship had left behind. "Look!"

"No, tell me!"

As the device rose higher off the ground, white electricity turned into an encasement of blue lightning. As everyone's hair stood on end, the mood of the crowd shifted to panic. Shouts rose, "Get back! Get back!"

John spun Evelyn around so she faced him. "Tell me the truth!" he insisted. "If I had insisted on going home — "

"Stop it! I told you, this is history in the making!" She patted his chest. "I'm my own person, John."

His face fell. "I just realized I'm not."

Heedless, Evelyn turned back to the spinning orb.

"Coming here isn't the problem," John said. "Knowing how much more you mean to me than I mean to you — "

Accompanied by a thunderous howl no human had ever heard before, blue arcs of lightning shot out from the device in all directions. Bolts seared human flesh and pierced multiple bodies in a growing chain of electric death.

A man with a thick Bronx accent shouted above the din, "Holy shit, it's a barbeque!"

As the screams of those attacked grew, the crowd panicked. The alien weapon burned and killed everything. Even the birds, the trees, and the insects were targets.

Everyone tried to flee what would come to be known as the Central Park Massacre. Only those at the very edges who ran fast and found their way to the tunnels beneath the city lived to tell the tale.

As the alien device discharged its lethal blasts, John and Evelyn fell backward behind the rock. As others rushed by, the couple did not dare move. If they stood to run, either the alien killing machine would murder them, or they'd be trampled in the crowd's mad stampede.

Lying flat on her back, Evelyn gazed straight up at the mother ship, still hovering high above the doomed city. Rapt, she could not take her eyes from the alien craft.

"Amazing," she muttered. "Amazing, amazing, amazing."

John had hit his head and was dazed from the fall. His ribs hurt because his wife had fallen atop him. His temple ached. Instinctively, he reached for the pain. When he pulled his hand away, it was wet with blood.

"Evy?"

Her gaze remained fixed on the spacecraft, seemingly afraid to blink, terrified of missing a moment. Undistracted by imminent death, she whispered in awe, "They came from the stars. They crossed unfathomable distances to find us."

He lay there, staring at his wife of nine years. They'd been high school sweethearts. They'd gone to the same school since they were children. She lay only an arm's length away, but she seemed as remote as a distant star.

I always said I'd go to the ends of the Earth for you, Evy, and it seems I have. I wonder if you'd even cross a street for me.

John had too much pride to admit the truth aloud, so he stayed silent. *Turn to me,* he thought. *Tell me you love me. Tell me you love me one more time, and I swear, I'll believe it. I really want to believe it because I love you so much!*

The alien weapon rose higher, expanding the circumference of its killing field.

Evelyn did not seem to hear him yell to her, nor did she grip his hand. She failed to tell him she loved him or even say goodbye. Evelyn died staring up at the warship that had come to destroy the human race.

John perished beside her, staring at her beautiful face.

II

Curiosity is the key to a locked door.
Not all doors should be opened.

CURIOSITY

Richard Issen thought his day was finally done, but the sky held secrets and the night ahead was to offer many terrors.

To save time, Richard had insisted on a meeting close to his apartment. However, with courtesy forced upon him, he had allowed the client to choose the restaurant. His business meeting had taken place at a high-end Indian restaurant. Unaccustomed to spicy food, he was eager to get to his bathroom.

As Richard set a brisk pace from the restaurant to his apartment building, the city's streets were jammed. Sirens howled in the distance. He passed a man and a woman shouting at each other in anger. With great effort, he doubled his pace, trotting past the couple. As the woman screamed, glass shattered behind him. Richard did not look back.

All these damn people, he thought. *Get rid of half of them, and we'd have twice as much peace and peace of mind.*

James, his doorman, was not at his station as Richard entered his apartment building. Judging by the flickering light behind the front desk, the small television James kept there was still on. However, the building's security was compromised. Richard made a mental note to complain to the property manager the next day. He declared to the empty lobby, "Intolerable incompetence. For all I pay in fees? Anyone could wander in here, for God's sake!"

With the madness of New York's nightlife behind him, he swiped his card for his private elevator. It carried Richard to his penthouse apartment, rising so fast his stomach lurched. Tapping one foot, he waited impatiently for the elevator to settle. The moment the doors parted, he burst into his living room and tossed his briefcase on the couch on the way to the toilet.

"Damned chutney," he muttered.

As soon as he sat down, he regretted leaving his briefcase on the couch. He would have to go over the contracts with the other senior partners early the next morning. He considered it a waste of time to relieve his trembling bowels without rereading the terms of the proposal. Sweating and grunting, Richard leaned forward to yank his phone from the pants puddled around his ankles.

"Hey, Siri! Call Desdemona Delvecchio."

Oddly, the call did not go through immediately. Richard kept trying with no success. He checked his watch. It was almost ten.

Surely she hadn't gone to bed yet, he thought. *I pay her enough. She knows to never turn her phone off.* He kept calling and finally got through.

She answered, "Dezzy D."

Richard sighed. She had to know who had called her. However, every time she insisted on wasting his time by announcing her ridiculous nickname.

"I need you to get in by seven a.m. sharp to set up the main conference room," Richard began. "It's too late for a caterer for breakfast, so you'll have to handle that. Croissants, bagels, and cream cheese will do for the breakfast meeting, but we'll be hammering out the Gordon v. Chevron file all day. Once you've loaded up the banquet table, call Easterby's about catering the lunch. Half sushi, vegan for Mr. Dale, and a steak and salad for me. The steak was not cooked enough last time. If it's pink, I will not be pleased."

He could hear her breathing, but she had not acknowledged any of his orders. "Desdemona? Tell me you wrote all that down. You know how I feel about repeating myself."

"Well, hello to you, too."

"Are you drunk?"

"Yep!"

"As long as you aren't nursing a hangover in the morning — "

"I won't be coming in tomorrow, Dick."

Dick? Richard thought. *She never calls me Dick. I've been Mr. Issen to every assistant I've ever had.*

"It's apparent you've been drinking too much."

"Really? I'd say I'm only half in the bag and not getting to the bottom of it nearly fast enough."

He sighed and before he could mute his phone, a wet fart began to escape, and he rushed to cover the device's microphone with the palm of his hand. Flushed with embarrassment, Richard took a moment to regain his composure. When he brought his cell back to his ear, his assistant was laughing uproariously.

"Was that you?" Richard demanded.

"You know it wasn't." Still laughing.

"Must be a bad connection."

"Yeah, right. As if you haven't called me from your porcelain throne ever since I took this lousy job."

Richard closed his eyes and took a few deep breaths before answering. "You know how I feel about vulgarity. Perhaps you've been working for me too long, Dezzy. You've never been so casual and familiar. How much alcohol was required to make you act so raucously? I expect a high level of decorum and professionalism from — "

"Oh, get over yourself."

"Miss Delvecchio? Has there been a coup?"

"Sorta. You haven't heard yet? I'm not coming in tomorrow. I bet no one is. I'm on the road with Derek right now. He's driving, I'm drinking."

Derek? Richard racked his brain. He vaguely recalled being introduced to her partner at last year's Christmas party. All this time Richard had thought the man's name was Dirk or possibly Darren.

"We can discuss your behavior at a more opportune time. These are important meetings," he said. "I've called the partners in, and if we don't keep up appearances, you will embarrass me."

"I didn't think you could be embarrassed. I guess you could blame me for anything that goes off the rails. Standard protocol is making you look good, right?"

Curiosity got the better of him. "Miss Delvecchio? Where do you think you're going?"

She laughed again, but this time her laughter had a bitter edge to it. "Where do I *think* I'm going?"

Richard heard her husband chuckle as she said, "Derek, honey? You won't believe this, but Mr. Issen wants to know where I *think* I'm going. That's a first. Since when do you suppose he cares what I think?"

"Since the end of the world," the man answered.

"We're headed north, Dick!" his assistant informed him. "Traffic's wall to wall and cheek by jowl, but my hubby's in the Air Force, so we got a head start. I told my friends hours ago what was coming. Please note, I did not call you. I've always wanted to call you Dick. Oh, no, that's not quite right. I always wanted to call you *a* dick. That's what we all call you behind your back. Dick Is-a-dick. Bye, you dick!"

The line went dead.

All? Richard thought. *What we all call you around the office?*

He didn't know what to do and that bothered him. Richard took pride in being the person who always knew what to do. He tried calling her back so he could fire her, but she did not pick up. He tried texting her, but the message remained undelivered.

When she sobers up, he thought, *she will be sorry.*

Richard resolved to get to the office even earlier than usual to have security pack up his assistant's personal belongings. In case she had been telling the truth about the firm's personnel calling him names behind his back, he would talk with HR. He would make sure a memo was sent out about gossip on the lower floors being a firing offense. And just to be certain he wasn't promoting a traitor, he'd require his next assistant be recruited from outside the firm.

"No one gets one over on Richard Issen," he proclaimed to his empty bathroom.

An irritating alarm sounded from his phone. Richard looked at the flashing screen in time to see: This is an alert from the Emergency Broadcast Sys —

The screen went dark, and a second or two later, the bathroom lights went out, too. Cursing and curious, Richard wanted to get off the toilet immediately. However, he was trapped there until his bowels finished their spasms. Richard attempted to restart his phone to find out what was happening, but the screen remained dark.

Somewhat confident his spicy meal had done all the damage it was going to do for the moment, Richard finally exited the bathroom. Emerging into his living room, he gazed out of the windows in shock. His penthouse usually offered an impressive view of the Brooklyn bridge. The city was darker than he'd ever seen it. The full moon was the only light.

Richard was in Manhattan in the blackout of July 2019. This was different from that, somehow eerier. It took him a moment to realize why. Power to the buildings was gone, sure, but where were the traffic headlights? The city's plunge into darkness had never been so complete.

The loss of power alone would have been disconcerting, but combined with the brief alert on his phone and his assistant's insubordination, Richard began to do something he thought was beneath him. Richard Issen began to worry. Desdemona had said her husband what's-his-name worked for the Air Force. What could he know that Richard did not?

"Terrorists," Richard said. "It's got to be terrorists."

Out of habit, he tried his phone again, hoping for more information. The device was still a useless hunk of metal, glass, and plastic. No power, no communication. With no one to complain to or to receive his orders, Richard was alone.

He went to the refrigerator for a bottle of water. Fumbling around in the dark, he found a bottle of Pellegrino with little difficulty. There wasn't much else in his fridge beside the water and white wine.

Richard returned to the bank of windows to stare out over the city. Somewhere between the restaurant, the hurried trip home, and the toilet, he'd sweated through his linen shirt. Moisture had sucked it to his back so he peeled it off and dropped it to the floor for the maid to deal with. He hoped the power outage would be over by morning. If the traffic lights were still out, the city would be at a standstill.

If this keeps going through tomorrow, no meetings for me.

At that thought, Richard experienced something new: a lack of urgency. He did not feel lonely. Dealing with other people — their foibles, their weaknesses, and their need for easy agreement — had always been a strain. His work and his accomplishments had always defined him. If he wasn't doing battle over a conference table, what was he?

Richard had been in his last year of law school when his firm scouted him. In the job interview, Richard told his interlocutor, "I am not a people person. I'm a numbers guy who only appreciates nuance in how to set the terms for a solid acquisitions contract. I can set traps in a contract, and I know how to get out of a bad deal."

Gene Calloway, the partner who had interviewed him, was now dead of a heart attack. For almost five years, Calloway repeated Richard's words from that job interview verbatim. "I'd never encountered a more confident asshole in my life," Gene would say. "As long as Richard is *our* asshole, I'm fine with it."

Richard felt as if he'd been running ever since, living up to his dogged reputation. He dated occasionally, but he'd failed to find a partner who tolerated the demands of his profession. Richard seldom had time for anyone who was not on his billable hours ledger.

Standing atop the darkened city, he felt lost and imagined he was the last man on Earth. He supposed he might eventually feel the need to be around others, but only if a painful cavity required filling from a helpful dentist.

This must be what peace feels like. I didn't expect things to get this quiet until they closed the coffin lid on me.

He didn't take peace for a good feeling. It was too unfamiliar. He decided to classify this experience as merely novel.

Maybe this is what it's like to be an Amish person at the end of a day. No phone, nothing to do but look at the stars and revel in a moment's pause from all the hard work. I should go to bed. Somewhere, an army of electricians is figuring out this mess.

As his jaw muscles relaxed and his shoulders dropped, Richard knew he should relax like this more often. Gene Calloway had promised himself to take up golf, lose weight and slow down. He didn't. That was about a month before his mentor died of cardiac arrest.

Lying in his hospital bed, Gene advised Richard to learn from his health crisis, "You're senior enough. You've earned the right to turn off the damn phone more often. Unplug from the rat race at least one day a week."

"Maybe I should have been born Amish," Richard had replied.

The next morning, Gene was dead. Richard promised himself to follow that good advice, but he did not. Instead, he took over all of Gene's files and closed three major mergers in the space of one year.

He was proud to be the man who knew what others did not, so curiosity nagged him. Instead of heading off to bed, he stood at the window to stare at the dead city, waiting for the lights to come back on.

Waiting for my life to begin again, he thought.

The outlines of skyscrapers made him think of tombstones. Without its lights, New York wasn't a moving, living thing anymore. Robbed of its power, it became a harbinger of the graveyard all cities eventually become.

What is going on? Nuclear attack? Dirty bomb? Missiles from North Korea on their way? God, what will this do to the stock market in the morning?

Richard did not receive an answer to his questions, but he got his first real clue when a passenger jet dropped from the sky. He did not see nor hear it until the aircraft exploded in a huge orange ball of flame. It shattered itself against the Brooklyn Bridge.

He froze. Death was something he heard about on the news. He hadn't seen a dead body since Gene Calloway's funeral. Before that, the only funeral he'd attended was that of his grandmother in England. To witness the explosion of a jet, knowing that he'd been present for the moment so many lives were extinguished shocked him. It was as if he'd been awakened by a cold bucket of water dumped on him. He backed away from the window, unable to tear his gaze from the burning wreckage. His phone was still useless, so it seemed there was nothing to do but bear witness to the accident.

Or is it an accident? He checked his assumptions. Something bigger than one airliner going down was happening. He wondered with whom the country would be at war tomorrow. Many of his stock holdings were investments in national defense. The mercenary part of his brain informed him that his portfolio was about to shoot up in value.

Transfixed by the flames, he regretted that thought. Innocent people were dead and he'd witnessed it. Richard didn't care for people, but that didn't mean he wished everyone ill. He only wanted the dumb ones to leave him alone.

Ray Issen, Richard's father, had always been a gregarious sort. He kept in touch with all his old friends and never missed an opportunity to be social. He expressed concern over his son's lifestyle and cantankerous attitude. "Wishing the dumb ones would leave you alone is the same as hating everyone."

"If true, that says more about them than me, Dad. I'm not you. I never feel lonely. For me, isolation isn't a curse. It's where I find safety. Now leave me alone."

He'd never returned to England to visit family since. Instead, he sent Christmas cards showing off the view from his penthouse. After the tragedy visited upon the city that night, bragging again about his high perch might appear in bad taste. How long would he have to wait before the bridge did not symbolize mass death? After the twin towers fell, Richard still could not look at New York's nightscape without feeling a couple of teeth were missing from the city's skyline.

Something on the bridge erupted in a secondary explosion, and Richard was horrified anew. Closing his eyes, he imagined people on the bridge who might still be alive. He imagined the screams and the smell of burning jet fuel.

After 9/11, New Yorkers came together, he thought. *Maybe that will happen again. The country needs that kind of unification now.*

In morbid fascination, Richard slid the glass door aside and stepped out onto his rooftop patio. As soon as the soundproof barrier was gone, he heard the shouts and screams. It seemed every nearby resident stood at their window to witness the flames rise from the shattered plane. People shouted from their balconies over and over, "Oh my God!" From what he could glean from their comments, they were no more informed than he.

No one is doing anything productive. But what was there to do?

The heated conversation he'd had with his assistant haunted him. What did her husband know? The man worked for the Air Force in some capacity, but Richard could not remember what he did. He hadn't gotten the impression the man was of high rank. For his assistant to treat him so shabbily as she fled the city, whatever warning they'd received must have been dire.

Something else bothered him, but he couldn't say exactly what. He closed his eyes and listened to the terrified voices rising out of the darkness of the wounded city. What was he missing?

Sirens, he thought. *Where are the sirens?*

No first responders were rushing to the scene. He went to the walls at the edge of his Japanese garden to peer into the streets below. No red, white, and blue lights flashed in any direction. He couldn't even spot the beam of a flashlight. It was as if all of New York had been thrown back into the Dark Ages.

He paced back and forth nervously for a few minutes before daring to take another peek at the streets below. Nothing changed but the rising alarm among his fellow citizens.

"Fellow citizens." He said it aloud with a tinge of disgust. The phrase haunted him. With his work and purpose stripped away, what was he? Just another one of the ordinary people, one of the masses yet devoid of any solid connection other than fear. Richard was unused to fear. Wealth and privilege had long insulated him from its cold touch.

As a child, Richard had been a loner. However, even for a person who reveled in solitude and privacy, this was too much. The thought that such an emergency could occur without authorities rushing to provide aid was startling. If emergency workers weren't coming for a disaster such as this, Richard truly was alone. If he needed help, no one would come for him. He didn't even have Desdemona to carry out his orders.

He went back to the wall at the edge of his garden and called out, "Does anyone know what is going on?"

No reply.

He tried again, louder this time, "I said, does anyone know what the hell is going on?"

People shouted to each other in the distance, but everyone ignored him. With the lights out, he'd become just another voice, another panicky know-nothing, easily ignored, not even acknowledged.

Richard couldn't stare at the burning wreckage on the Brooklyn Bridge anymore. There seemed to be no point. There was no one to tell. Richard was no longer a god high above the city. Instead, in a matter of minutes, he'd become a hermit on a mountaintop, too remote and beyond reach. This was a revelation for a man who'd thought of himself as needing no one yet so necessary to others.

This must be loneliness. I've never felt it to this depth.

Aside from the flames, the only visible light was the moon and the stars. Devoid of light pollution, the night sky seemed a sudden thing, as if a dark cloak had been pulled aside to reveal secrets.

When was the last time I saw the stars?

He couldn't remember when he even looked skyward. Perhaps on his first and last trip to Wales. There'd been a girl there. He'd met Heather in a bookshop. She liked hiking, and he said he did, too, even though he didn't. He'd enjoyed his time with her, though. It was the only time he'd camped overnight.

She seemed to like him, but when he left her at the bus stop to return to school, he never heard from her again. Richard stalked her on Facebook occasionally. She still lived in Hay-on-Wye. Each year, Heather volunteered at the book festival. She married a plumber and had three children. In the photos, they all looked happy.

He pictured Heather standing beside him in his rooftop garden. Richard paid someone else to tend it. If Heather had followed him to America and become his wife, perhaps she would take care of raking the garden. Richard would be holding her now, pretending to be strong for her. She would love and respect him because, more than most, he was in control of his world.

In his fantasy, Heather did not age. She was still the girl from Wales who knew how to zip two sleeping bags together so they were one under the twinkling stars.

Richard imagined himself the hero, but he knew he wasn't. He'd rushed past that couple arguing in the street earlier. He hadn't even looked back when he heard glass shattering. He could use his fluttering intestines and spicy food as his excuse as to why he rushed on. Deep down in a place he rarely dared to look, he knew he would have passed them by no matter the circumstances.

Richard gave a helpless shrug. Whispering to the stars, more of his native accent crept in than he normally allowed. "I could say I'm not a people person, but I'm just kind of shite. Dezzy and everyone at the office knows. Even way back when, Heather knew I was never any good with people. I am one, but you'd have to look close to say for sure. Sorry."

As if in answer, a bright white light appeared directly overhead. At first, he took it for a helicopter, but he heard no whirring rotors, and there was no wind. It was farther away than he first thought, but whatever it was descended upon him quickly.

His jaw went slack as he stared up in awe. In the distance, people screamed and shouted again, but their words were indistinct. Richard couldn't hear them over the roar of his pulse pounding in his ears.

The bright white light grew larger and larger, seeming to encompass everything. Richard shielded his eyes with his hands, but even through closed eyelids, he could see the bones of his hands.

Jesus, it's the eye of God, and I'm not ready to die.

Richard cried out for his mother as he collapsed into the warm relief of unconsciousness.

Richard awoke in a windowless gray room made entirely of metal. Struggling to focus, he looked up to find the walls were curved. One side was a black screen, but no door was evident.

Behind him, a woman said, "Finally."

Richard sat up and turned. The woman sat with her back against the wall. She was barefoot, but otherwise clad in brown leather. Her heavy red lipstick was smeared, and her hair was mussed. She seemed displeased with him.

"How long was I out?"

She shrugged. "No watch, no phone. How am I supposed to know?"

"What happened?"

"We've been taken."

"By whom?"

She shrugged. "I woke up next to you a while ago. I poked you, but you kept on dreaming."

"Dreaming?"

"You were talking in your sleep. You drunk?"

He shook his head and got to his feet with some difficulty. He sniffed the air. "Something smells good. Smells like — what is that?"

"Ginger cookies, maybe?" she suggested.

"I'm reminded of squares my mother used to make."

In three paces, Richard stood at the screen, searching for a seam. Finding nothing, he pressed on it. If there was a way out, he couldn't figure out how the exit worked.

"Tried that already," the woman said.

"No luck?"

"Obviously."

"Have I offended you in some way?" Richard asked.

She shook her head. "Not yet. Excuse me if I'm a little on edge. This is my first kidnapping."

"I'm Richard Issen. What's your name?"

"Penelope Chang. Professor Penelope Chang. I teach online courses at NYU. What do you do?"

"Lawyer. Mergers and acquisitions mostly."

"You *were* a lawyer. I think our professions have suddenly become irrelevant."

"I'm not ready to retire yet," he said. "Fill me in. The lights went out. There was a plane crash. A passenger jet exploded when it hit the Brooklyn Bridge. Did you see it?"

She shook her head.

"Last I remember, I was at my penthouse apartment. There was a big bright white light. After that ... well, here I am."

"I was at Coopers Beach, Southampton."

"Really? Working at NYU, I assumed you'd be in the city."

"I was working remotely from a friend's cottage. We were walking along the beach when I saw the invasion begin."

Richard stared at her a moment. "Invasion?"

"It rose out of the water."

"From the *water*?"

"That's what I said, because that's what I saw. Do you lack imagination, Mr. Issen?"

"Please tell me more, Ms. Chang."

"Not much to tell. It was an armada that went from swimming to flying. Alien aircraft, big and bulky. I saw at least half a dozen of them before I blacked out."

"UFOs?" Little else made sense, but he found he could not rein in his skeptical tone. "You're claiming we were captured by aliens in a UFO?"

"I'm guessing that's generally how they travel. Aliens would look mighty strange on a bus."

"Wow."

"Does this look like a courtroom, sir? I'm not 'claiming' anything, by the way. I'm saying it."

"There has to be another explanation."

"Does there? Why?"

Richard found himself at a loss for words, struggling to come up with something else that made sense. He didn't really doubt her, but he wished for a more comfortable answer. Finally, he asked, "Why did you think these aircraft were of alien origin?"

Penelope straightened and swept her hair from her eyes. "Several reasons. First, a bunch of these vehicles rose out of the Atlantic and into the air. Can you think of anything else that can manage that?"

"A missile from a submarine."

"A missile as big as a bunch of football stadiums piled on top of each other? That's kind of what they looked like, but they weren't uniform, either."

Richard's thoughts raced. Military vehicles often looked alike. If there was some variance in these massive vehicles, he hoped that meant their purpose was not aggressive.

When he shared that idea, Professor Chang was not encouraging. "We've been taken against our will by an unknown force. You think the idea of aliens is crazy, but the only other explanation I have is Atlanteans. That sounds much less likely, doesn't it? You're one of those guys who like to think he's rational. Searching for confirmation bias isn't that, Mr. Issen."

Richard thought of all the recordings of unexplained craft chased by Navy pilots. At the time, it was nothing more than a fun news item with which one of the junior partners was obsessed. UAPs or Unidentified Aerial Phenomena, he'd called it. Richard wrote it off as top secret experimental aircraft, probably drones.

"We've never met," Professor Chang said. "Why would aliens want me and a pudgy, shirtless middle-aged lawyer? If they think we're going to mate and make offspring for their human zoo, joke's on them! My baby-making factory got removed two decades ago."

To conceal his anger, Richard turned back to the black screen. To conceal his flabby middle, he sucked in his gut. "I can't wait to ask them what this is about. Tell me, what do you teach, Professor? I'm guessing it's not diplomacy and interplanetary relations."

"Anthropology," she replied.

"Ah, so you're a conversationalist. If you were a little nicer, I bet you'd be good at cocktail parties."

"Pardon me?"

"Anthropology? Really? It's a degree that's useless other than to teach it. Anthropologists make nothing more than other anthropologists."

To his surprise and disappointment, she laughed at his attempt to insult her. "Well, you're not all wrong there. My plight could be worse, though. I could be a half-naked corporate lawyer who has never read *How to Win Friends and Influence People*."

"I've read *Winning Through Intimidation* and *The Art of War* a few times."

A thump came from behind the black screen. Richard and the professor went silent, straining to hear more. When nothing more happened, Penelope let out a guffaw. "I'm terrified and curious in equal parts. Never felt that way before."

"I think I'm a little more scared than curious," Richard admitted, "but I'm with you."

"Imagine my relief," she replied.

Finally, a dim dot of yellow light came on in the center of the screen.

"Something's happening. I wonder if they get *Desperate Housewives*," she wondered aloud.

Richard rolled his eyes. "If they judge us by our reality television shows, we're screwed."

A high chittering sound came from behind the screen, and the yellow dot turned to bright green and expanded until it filled the screen from floor to ceiling.

Bathed in the green glow, Richard called out, "Hello? Is anyone there?"

"And can you get him a shirt?" Penelope asked.

Richard gave her a withering stare. "Really? Now?"

She shrugged. "Just trying to add a little levity to ... whatever this is. Also, I'd be more comfortable if you wore a shirt."

"Me, too," Richard said.

"Me, too," a deep voice interjected from behind the screen.

Penelope and Richard looked at each other. "Are they mimicking me, or — "

"I understand you perfectly," the voice said.

Penelope stood. "Why have you taken us? We want to go home."

"Your trip aboard our ship will be over soon."

That sounds ominous, Richard thought. However, he decided to pursue answers instead of fear. "Why have you taken us prisoner?"

After a long pause, the deep voice answered, "We have been monitoring your species for some time, and I wished to meet a couple of your kind up close."

Penelope crossed her arms. "I don't buy it. With the distances involved, you can't be aliens. You're from our future, aren't you? Come back to fix things, I'm guessing? Yes? No? Maybe so?"

The high chittering sounded again. The voice soon returned. "We are not human, I assure you."

"Then how do you speak our language?" Penelope asked.

"That's right!" Richard pounced. "Quite the coincidence that you speak perfect English. *I* have more of a discernible accent than you!"

The chitter sounded again, and the screen turned dark red. "We have had plenty of time to learn your languages from afar as we traveled. Our scouts have been on the planet for a long time."

The planet, Richard thought. The alien did not say *your* planet.

"Ah," the professor said. "Of course."

"Of course? Of course what? This makes no sense!" Richard prided himself on calm rationality. Despite his best efforts, the timbre of his voice had begun to climb higher, toward the edge of hysteria.

Penelope glared at him. "Doesn't it? An alien race has the technological capacity to cross the galaxy to come to Earth. You don't think they have the tech to listen to our broadcasts and pick up our lingo? Use your noodle and adapt to new information, man."

Richard thought again of those videos by Navy pilots. Though he'd dismissed those recordings before as curiosities, the fast-moving craft suddenly seemed more threatening. "So they *are* aliens," he said. "*Hmph!* Why? Because they said so?"

"Because we're powerless," she replied. "They have no reason to lie. What do they care what a lawyer and an anthropologist think of them?" Penelope turned to the screen. "So, Mr. Alien, what do you want?"

"I am just one of a crew, a biologist. You were selected at random for the benefit of my curiosity."

Penelope went back to her place on the floor and leaned against the wall. "You've already been monitoring us. What do you need to know? How a bill becomes a law? Or perhaps you want my Aunt Edie's pancake recipe. Makes it just like IHOP."

Richard whirled on her. "Can't you take this seriously?"

Penelope shook her head. "I think this will go easier if we keep our sense of humor. It's an invasion by a species of superior technical capabilities. Ask any indigenous person how they fared when colonizers packing more advanced weaponry arrived."

Richard winced and through gritted teeth snarled, "Don't give them any ideas!"

The chittering resumed and went on for a long time. When the alien voice returned, it was somewhat different, a little higher in tone. "We didn't understand IHOP, but another of the crew did get the reference."

Richard turned back to the screen. "You're using a machine to simulate human speech, aren't you? And that's someone different. How many are you, anyway?"

A moment of silence stretched out before the answer came. "There are three of us behind the screen, but our ships hold many."

Penelope smiled. "Guarded answers. They don't want to give away any military secrets. This is a military mission. We're definitely screwed."

"This machine speaks for us. Our biology does not allow us to simulate human speech," the alien continued.

Richard and Penelope exchanged nervous glances.

"Almost every alien I've ever seen depicted in movies and on TV is pretty much human," Richard said.

"If we're that different," Penelope said, "it'll be easier for them to give even less of a shit about us. People resonate with people who look like them. I bet that's universal."

Richard objected, "You can't know that — "

"No, the female is correct," the alien interjected. "We choose not to show ourselves to you because you are fragile. On the few occasions we have revealed ourselves, your kind became less rational."

Penelope stood, suddenly energized. "So you've taken people before."

"Our scouts have, yes, for study."

A small hope began to blossom over Richard's heart. There were plenty of stories of alien abduction, but they always occurred in some remote area. The abductees were usually less than credible. If they'd abducted other humans and returned them to Earth unharmed, he still had hope of surviving this ordeal. "What did you learn from those previous abductions?"

"Human anatomy and physiology. Primates are fascinating."

"If you're planning on probing me," Penelope said, "I do not consent. Not on the first date, anyway."

"Why would you need to know anything about our anatomy?" Richard asked.

The professor answered for the alien. "To make them better killers when they take over. Or is it more like collecting butterflies and pinning them to a board?"

Some chittering went back and forth behind the screen. Finally, a deep voice replied, "You, the female. Impressive, though you should know, we did not abduct nearly as many humans as stories in your popular culture would have you believe."

"Mostly legend," Penelope said. "Nailed it, but I'm not sure that makes much difference one way or the other now. God, I want a cigarette, a coffee, and I want it to be Sunday morning. Just me, the New York Times crossword, and my corgi at my feet."

Richard's breathing suddenly became shallow. He found he had to sit on the cold floor. "This..." He panted. "This is unacceptable. I will not stand for this."

"Literally, apparently." Penelope let out a bitter laugh. "Calm down and begin to slow your breaths. Cup your hands and breathe into them. You're hyperventilating."

"This ... should ... not ... be ... happening ... to me."

"But it's okay that I'm kidnapped?"

Richard shook his head. Following the professor's advice, his breathing was slowing. Her advice worked and he hated her for it.

After a couple of minutes, she asked if he felt better, and he gave her a grudging nod.

"Not used to speed bumps, are you? Gotta tell you, man, for the rest of us who've had to struggle, this is no surprise. People like me expect everything to go wrong. Things are often so bad, when things go right for me, I get nervous."

"An anthropology professor who spends her Sundays doing the New York Times crossword has it rough."

"Not that titles, power, and privilege mean much now, but I wasn't always a professor. Guys like you, when you fall, you fall farther."

Richard lay on one side and curled up into the fetal position. "You're taking the invasion of Earth well."

She shrugged. "Not really, but see this?" She gestured to her face. "This is what you call a brave front. I'd do even better if I had a cigarette, but my pack ran dry. If I'd known it was Alien Abduction Night, I would have made sure I had a fresh pack on me. Hey? Hey! Get up. You're embarrassing me in front of the alien conquerors. Have some dignity, man!"

Richard forced himself to stand up. *I'm a great lawyer,* he thought. *I never spoke in front of the Supreme Court, but I could have. I can talk my way out of this. Earth needs a diplomat and here I am.*

Richard turned toward the screen. "What is it you want from us? If we can figure that out together, I'm sure we can come to an equitable solution."

The chittering behind the screen went on and on.

Richard looked to the professor. "Are they conferring, do you think?"

"Whenever they make that sound, I suspect they're laughing." Penelope got up and strode to the screen to rap on it sharply. "Hey! I have questions for you!"

"I was opening a dialogue," Richard said. "What are you doing?"

"You said you read *The Art of War*. Wasn't there something in there about knowing your enemy? Wasn't that a huge point of the thing?"

She kept rapping on the screen until the alien voice returned. "This could prove interesting. What are your questions?"

"You've been around? Like, here on Earth? Where've you been hiding?"

"We have created environments that suit us in your oceans."

"Do you have gills?" Richard ventured.

The aliens chittered again behind the screen. Richard winced at the high grind of that noise.

"No, we do not have gills. Our environments are sustained beside hydrothermal vents."

Richard suddenly reenergized. A dialogue had been established. "Aha! So you've been hiding in the deep sea!"

"Obviously," the alien replied dryly. "It is remarkable that your kind seems so fascinated with missions to planets within your solar system. A few of you spend immense resources on very limited technology. Space travel far beyond your atmosphere would inevitably end in death for any of you foolish enough to attempt such manned exploration. Meanwhile, the vast majority of your planet that is underwater remains unexplored."

"But that's just it!" Richard enthused. "We breathe a mix of what? Nitrogen and oxygen, right? If you have to live beside a hydrothermal vent — "

"You guys breathe methane?" Penelope asked.

"A richer mix than is currently in your atmosphere, yes."

Richard trembled with excitement. "Yeah! Methane! Right! So living above the surface isn't going to work for you! How about a

compromise? You can have the oceans, and we'll leave you alone. I'm not in charge of these things, but I know people who know people —
"

The professor scoffed. "They're a technologically superior alien race who found their way here from God-knows-where. You don't think they know they can't breathe our air?"

The chittering returned and Richard was embarrassed again. His fellow prisoner was smug and unhelpful, but he was almost sure she was right. The aliens found him amusing. "These bastards are laughing at the monkeys in the zoo," he muttered.

The professor clapped him on the back. "Now you're getting it, big guy. I knew you'd catch up eventually."

"Your planet is ripe for remodeling to our purposes. We can accelerate the release of methane from the tundra. After several years of resetting the planet's gaseous mixture, we will be able to exit our ships without any protective equipment — "

"Before you know it, an alien will be living in your fancy penthouse, Richard," Penelope said. "Of course, you won't know it at all. You and I and everybody else will be long dead. I thought we'd be teetering on extinction within three generations, anyway." Penelope shrugged. "Maybe it's not the great loss you think it is. It's not like we were killing it. Couldn't even say we had a good run."

Richard gazed into the woman's eyes. "Are you literally crazy?"

"I'm a realist who suffers from depression and deals with it by smoking and drinking too much. What's it to you? It's not like anything matters much anymore. Did you have big plans to turn your life around and go save the whales or something?"

Richard took two quick strides to the screen and pounded on it with his fists. "C'mon out! Show yourselves! You're nothing but a bunch of bullies and cowards, aren't you? Aren't you?"

Penelope mocked him. "Ooh, kitty has claws!"

"Quiet, you!"

"I don't believe you can make a bargain with alien creatures who flew all this way. I mean, what have you got to offer them? They're obviously not happy with the status quo. Getting frustrated and putting on a show probably isn't going to help either. What's your plan? Fistfight for the future of the planet? Winner takes all?"

Richard whirled on her. "What have you got to contribute?"

Penelope twisted her lips and seemed to take his challenge seriously. Bobbing her head, she turned back to the screen. "Is the flabby old lawyer right? Are you afraid to show yourselves?"

"We provide this chamber for you because it is vented to your atmosphere. You could not breathe on this side of the barrier. Also, humans find our appearance so foreign that reasonable conversation is often useless — "

"Challenge accepted!" Penelope said.

There was a long pause before the alien asked her to clarify her statement.

"You're big and bad? I want to face my executioner. Is the lawyer right? Are you a bunch of cowards?"

"We assure you, you do not have the capacity to harm us. You are as harmless as children."

"My little nephew head-butted me once," Penelope muttered. "Almost lost two front teeth."

Richard swore at their captors and more chittering sounded from behind the screen.

"There are gaps in understanding between your kind and ours," the deep voice said. "We do not recognize the concept of cowardice. We make choices or we do not. Such empty value judgments carry no weight here."

Penelope gave Richard a sly grin. "Told you they were more advanced."

Richard sat on the floor again and put his head in his hands. "What do you bastards want from us?"

Penelope knew that answer, too. "Rich, I don't want you to get more upset, but what do you think the two of us can offer an alien race bent on the destruction of the human race? C'mon, think it through. Unless you have the cheat codes to shut down missile command, the answer is pretty obvious."

He didn't look up. Richard could only shake his head in disbelief at how quickly his life had turned to disaster. "I don't want to know."

"They're aliens who've been living at the bottom of the ocean, Richard," she said softly. "But I doubt they're pescatarians."

"The woman is correct," the higher alien voice said. "You are meat."

Richard began to weep. Penelope's face softened, and she knelt beside him, whispering in his ear, "It'll be okay. This will all be over soon, and you won't feel a thing, or at least not for long at all. I promise."

"When we drop the barrier," the alien said, "our atmosphere will flood the chamber. You will not be able to breathe for long. We will allow you a moment to see your ... replacements. You will find this interesting, we are sure, and we are not without courtesy. We are kind, even to our herds."

"Alien shit!" Richard spat. "Hell, *I'm* going to be alien shit. When all is said and done, I guess that's not much worse than what I was. What have I done with my life? I should have stayed in Wales!"

"Oh, c'mon," Penelope said. "I was just stressed and joshing before. You can't be that bad."

"People who know me best would disagree. I was awful to my assistant, and I never apologized. With no control of things ... what's left? What's worse, I figured this out too late. I'll never get the chance to be a better person!"

"You're in a good place to end on, Richard."

"Huh?"

"I mean, screw it. What do we need to hang around for? Chin up, man! I've studied history. Everything ends. Embrace change. Help me out here. I'm nervous, too. C'mon, brave face, remember? Let's show them we can go out in defiant dignity. Don't give them the satisfaction, right?"

He clutched at her hand. "You're right. I know you're right."

Penelope whispered to Richard, "We're going to see real live aliens before we die. Isn't it exciting? No line to this exhibit so it's already better than Disney."

"You are a little crazy."

"A little crazy is what's called for," she said.

Richard lifted his head in time to see the screen drop to the floor. His eyes widened as he struggled to comprehend what he beheld.

The screen was in two layers. The first opaque layer slid smoothly to the floor to reveal a transparent screen.

Three aliens stood there. He'd seen depictions of aliens, of course, but none like this. Their skin was scaly like that of a reptile, but their torsos appeared to be a segmented carapace like that of a crab. Richard couldn't decide if they were naked or if the aliens wore armor. Their heads resembled that of cephalopods.

Octopi, Richard thought. *I'm about to be butchered by an octopus! I worked so hard to get everything I thought I wanted. This is what it all comes down to.*

"Wow," Penelope said. She trembled. "Are you seeing what I'm seeing?"

"Katharine Hepburn," Richard replied.

"What?"

"I'm thinking of the actress."

"What about her?"

"She collected a bunch of stuff from her films. Dresses, ashtrays ... whatever."

"You've lost me," Penelope said.

"When she died, they held a huge estate auction. I remember thinking at the time that aside from some great films almost no one sees anymore, she was erased. No matter how large we loom, ultimately, we're erased. A blip. I feel like a blip. Just this afternoon, everything felt so important. *Everything!*"

"Richard, I get it. But listen to me, there's still something important to do. When they drop the screen, hold your breath so you can see. They're the future and we are about to be part of history. Okay, big guy? When they open up, quick deep breath!" Penelope said.

"Why?" Richard asked.

"Because I don't want to do this alone."

Tears slid down his cheeks as Richard squeezed her hand. He even managed a small smile of commiseration.

The transparent screen rose to the ceiling as a vent behind them opened and began to hiss as their air began to seep out slowly.

One of the aliens lifted a device to its mouth, a vertical slit surrounded by short tentacles. "You will not suffer."

Penelope produced a cigarette lighter from her palm. Richard's eyes widened as she flicked its small steel wheel and lit a flame.

Richard Issen's last thought was, *Methane! Yes! Take that, you murderous bastards!*

Penelope Chang's last thought was, *I finally quit smoking.*

There was still just enough oxygen to ignite the ship's atmosphere. Fire raged through the alien ship, climbing from chamber to chamber as if the flame itself was unconfined rage. After several explosions ripped through the craft, it dropped from the sky. The spaceship crushed acres of forest beneath its hull.

It was only one ship in the alien armada. Their sacrifice did not even give the invasion pause. However, Penelope was right. Our choices are few. As we each meet our end, we may opt for whining desperation or dignified acceptance. We may even choose defiance.

Perhaps there are no cowards or heroes, only actions, reactions, and choices. The moments before death is our last chance to choose.

Penelope and Richard chose defiance.

III

Prolific authors are everywhere.
That sounds nice, but you'll see what I really mean with the next story.

EVERYONE IS AN AUTHOR

Major Boaz Melamed of the 48th Airlift Squadron passed through three security checkpoints before taking the massive freight elevator down. The Vault lay ninety feet below the Little Rock Air Force Base, Melamed's orders were to report to Colonel Hannah Fresco. He'd traveled through darkened streets to get to the base. Stepping off the elevator, he was relieved to find the Vault's hallways brightly lit.

Tonight, I'll take any semblance of normalcy, no matter how fragile.

He'd never been down to the Vault. A baby-faced young corporal named Harrison eagerly escorted Melamed to Fresco's office. "Did you hear they attacked New York, sir?"

"I did not. What's the word on the Underground?"

"Scattered reports. Well, just one report really. I got a buddy down in Communications. He says it all sounds like a movie, but this is not a drill."

"Slow your trot, Corporal. You're running the rumor mill too hard. Don't want to spread panic."

"Yes, sir, sorry, sir. I wouldn't tell anyone off base."

"You're panicking *me*, Harrison."

"Oh. Sorry, sir."

As they arrived at the CO's door, Melamed leaned close to the corporal's ear. "Go do penance and clean a latrine. Once you've repented, go get some sleep and start fresh tomorrow. I'm told tomorrow is another damned day."

Colonel Fresco's office door was open. As the major peered in, he found his superior officer at her desk bent over a sheet of paper, making notes. She looked to be fiftyish, white-haired, and harried. Hurriedly making notes by a single desk lamp, she reminded him of his older sister studying late into the night to become a doctor.

Without looking up, she told him to enter. "I've been expecting you, Major. Have a seat. Let's skip the formalities and introductions. We're in a race against time, and I need your input. We have captured one of them."

Melamed's eyes widened in disbelief. "How was that accomplished, Colonel? The sergeant who picked me up said he had to change out his Jeep's battery. Little Rock's in chaos after a flyover by a massive UAP. I barely made it here through city streets."

"Why? What's going on up there."

"The civvies are out in force, partying like it's the end of the world."

"They might have the right idea. Our information is that it is the end of the world, Major. It's certainly the end of the world as we know it."

"And we've got an alien? Here? On site?"

"I understand the confusion and excitement but dial it back. Keep it under your hair, but three generals are in the Officer's Mess getting hammered. I've got more than a few AWOL airmen and technicians. Not that I don't understand the impulse. They've read the tea leaves."

Melamed tried to maintain his facade of cool professionalism, but at that news, he could not maintain his poker face. "AWOL, ma'am?"

"Yeah, there's a real *Dr. Strangelove* vibe around here since we started getting the radios working again. These ships appeared in random places. It's almost as if they don't give a shit about the borders on our maps. It's all just a planet for them to dominate, I guess. Seems there's plenty strange going on and we don't have the full picture. For instance, I just found out a frigate sent out a strange distress call. The Navy seems to have lost track of it."

"Careless of them, ma'am," Melamed cracked.

She appeared annoyed, so the major gave her a nod of contrition. "Sorry, Colonel. This is just a lot to take in."

"It'll get worse long before it gets better. Here's what you need to know. Sometime last evening, one of the alien ships crashed. Evidence on the ground was that some sort of fire ignited something or other onboard and here we are. Fortunately, the crash site was in the woods of upstate New York, so the damn thing didn't kill anybody on the ground, at least that we know of. Unfortunately, the soldiers on the recovery mission got a little overexcited and shot several survivors before they remembered their heads. The recovery team insists they didn't hurt the detainee, so it must have been injured in the crash."

"Upstate New York? How did our people even get there?"

"I've got one shielded C-130 that managed to land at Mitchel Field."

"Shielded, Colonel?"

"The nerd squad tells me it was an EMP burst. For almost a minute, we assumed the blackout was confined to the Eastern Seaboard. It's not. The power outage is global."

Melamed was in awe. "Unprecedented."

"At least we're sure it's not a foreign power that did this to us. The tech is too high to be of earthbound origin. Computer and TV networks are knocked out, and there's still a bunch of the populace who don't know what's going on. They're still sitting at home waiting for their Facebook accounts to come back up so they can complain to somebody."

He gave her a smile, but her gaze remained fixed on the paper on the desk. She held up one finger and made another note. "Jesus, I hope you can read my writing. I type. I can't remember the last time I wrote anything with a pen with the exception of my signature."

"The computers are knocked out, even all the way down here, Colonel?"

"We were spared the EMP burst. Anything deep enough underground or sitting in a Faraday cage was unaffected. I'm keeping this on paper for operational security." She gestured to the papers on her desk. "Back to that in a minute.

"Here's what we know about the EMP burst: The enemy's device wasn't a nuke, but it's exponentially stronger than our best experimental pinch."

"Pinch, ma'am?"

"Pinch, meaning a device that can knock out electrical systems in a single burst. For obvious reasons, we're having a hard time getting reports from far and wide. What we know so far is it seems to have fried electronic devices, and the impact is both ubiquitous and comprehensive. From your electric shaver to your wife's dildo, if it had a battery in it, toss it in recycling."

"I'm single, ma'am, but I'll be sure to toss *my* dildo in recycling when I get home."

"*If* you get home. That's a long-odds bet at the moment. I hear you served in Guantanamo."

"Yes, Colonel. Interrogations."

"Enhanced or soft?"

"Enhanced was overblown and didn't work. I worked soft."

"I'm told you were good at it."

"I got actionable intelligence the sadists did not get, ma'am, yes. One guy spilled his guts after I sang a song with him from his childhood."

"Uh-huh. Look, I heard you had a smart mouth. You better have a smart brain to go with it. One level down, the prisoner is waiting for you." Fresco handed the paper to him. "Here are my questions. You have until dawn. By then brass from Area 6 will show up and take it away from us."

"Not Area 51?" He regretted asking as soon as the question popped out of his mouth.

"Area 51 is for the tourists and freaks to hassle. Area 6 is where all the unmanned aerial vehicle testing is going on. They're trying to rejig and accelerate their program in light of recent events. Personally,

I think moving the enemy combatant around is a waste of time. Area 6 will soon be irrelevant."

He scanned the list. "What question is your top priority, Colonel?"

"Just one? If I had to choose one, it would be how do we take down the other alien craft. Get all you can. Things are looking grim, Major. We don't have much capacity for kinetic action, so by this time tomorrow, I suspect we'll be using nukes on the invasion force."

"Missile silos were not affected, ma'am?"

"Negative. They're *underground*."

"Right. Yes, ma'am."

"However, those weapons are already warmed up. A serious contingent at the Pentagon are already pushing to go hot immediately."

"What about our subs, Colonel?"

"Also cocked and ready to rock, but at the moment, we are unclear on targeting. For instance, how many enemy UAPs are there? We have no idea. Last count was thirty-seven, including the one that somehow made it all the way across the galaxy, but somehow couldn't negotiate power lines or something."

"Unfathomable."

"Fathom it. There is a weakness there somewhere, and we need to know how to exploit it. It's your job to find anything of tactical use. Keep the singing to a minimum. This isn't a journey of cultural discovery. We need intel to develop a coherent strategy."

Melamed took another moment to scan the questions. "We need to understand their objectives, lethal capacity, and troop movements."

"Go discuss it with the prisoner. It speaks English better than anyone on my staff. Most of my staff are idiots, but it's still impressive."

Melamed had many questions and clarifications, but he was too eager to speak with the detainee from outer space. Halfway out the door, he froze for a moment, then spun on his heel. "Colonel, one question, if I may?"

"Major?"

"Am I authorized to discuss terms of surrender?"

"If they're the ones doing the surrendering, sure."

The same corporal who had escorted him to Colonel Fresco's office waited for him in the hallway.

"Did you clean your latrine, Harrison?"

"I was quick, sir. The colonel's orders were to stay close by and escort you to the SCIF. We lifted the alien's room right out of the wreckage and put it directly on the C-130. All the while, Cinnamon just stood there like a tree."

"Uh ... Cinnamon? *What?*"

"That's what the Marines who brought it in call it, sir. It smells like the spice."

"Linear, but visceral. Has the prisoner been examined by Medical?"

"No, sir. Captain Frank and his team are examining the corpses of two bodies they recovered."

"I was told the prisoner was injured."

"Captain Frank says he doesn't have enough of a baseline to do anything for the prisoner. He said, and I quote, 'How am I supposed to get a blood pressure on that thing, and how would I know what's normal and what's not?'"

"It's that different from us, huh?"

The corporal wiped a bead of sweat from his brow. He looked haunted. "That, and confidentially, sir, I doubt he wanted to get close to the thing. You'll see, sir, the prisoner is like something out of a horror movie. Almost shit my pants first time I saw it."

"Good thing I'm freshly shat. What else?"

"The thing breathes a mix of oxygen, nitrogen, and methane. It can breathe our atmosphere but would prefer a richer mix of methane."

"And how do we know that precisely?"

"Cinnamon told us, Major. Its looks could stop a truck and make my mama cry, but it's as polite as a Southern gentleman nursing a mint julep. Leastways, that's what the colonel had to say about it."

The pair went down one flight of stairs and passed two more checkpoints before entering a large concrete room. Three cameras pointed at a tall square box that stood in front of the freight elevator. Three sides of the box were slate gray. The wall facing the cameras was transparent. Spotlights bathed the prisoner in bright white light.

The alien had been facing the rear of its cell but turned at his approach. Major Melamed stopped short at the sight of it. He'd once been on an elevator when a young woman with a facial deformity stepped on. Unprepared, he'd taken in a sharp involuntary gasp at the shock. Embarrassed, he'd quickly apologized. The woman smiled her understanding, and no more words were exchanged. Oddly, he had a similar reaction to seeing the alien for the first time, as if he'd glimpsed something awful he wasn't supposed to acknowledge.

The alien's thorax reminded him of an ant's body. The skin was reptilian, but the oversized head was bulbous, like that of an octopus. A few tendrils around the vertical slit of a mouth reinforced that impression. He guessed the beast stood almost seven feet tall. It appeared bipedal, but four arms sprouted from the thorax. On closer inspection, it appeared one of the arms was not symmetrical. It was bent at an odd angle. Melamed guessed that was the injury the prisoner had sustained in the crash.

He counted seven fingers plus what he took for a very long thumb on each hand. The sight made his stomach churn. *How am I supposed to establish rapport and get intelligence from a thing so different from a human?*

But it was the large yellow eyes that made him cold with shock. They were as big as ostrich eggs and without pupils. The alien did not blink. Instead, a shiny wet film covered them. Melamed felt compelled to meet the alien's gaze. The Air Force officer felt somehow gathered in by it.

Those grotesque eyes! Almost hypnotic. And what if those aren't even Cinnamon's eyes? What if I'm staring at its balls? The absurdity of the situation gave Melamed the courage to move closer.

Four guards with AR-15s stood watch. The major had been so focused on the alien, he hadn't noticed the other humans in the room. He ordered them all back behind the cameras.

"Do you need anything from me, sir?" the corporal asked. "Coffee?"

"No, thank you, Corporal. I think my nerves are amped up sufficiently already. Didn't I say something about you getting some sleep earlier? Scat. If I need anything, I'll get one of these guys on it."

The corporal thanked Melamed and scurried toward the exit. Harrison appeared very glad to get out of the room.

Melamed ignored the cameras and the chair set beside them. He stalked straight to the prisoner. "I am Major Boaz Melamed. I'm here to interview you."

The alien bent its massive head to look him up and down. The movement seemed to confirm that they were indeed meeting each other's gaze. Cinnamon took a beat before speaking clearly in perfect English, "*Hello, Clarice.*"

Melamed was struck speechless for a moment. It passed through his mind that he might be the target of a truly elaborate prank. However, he stood his ground lest this was some kind of test and the alien think him weak.

"Funny. You're screwing with me," Melamed said. "People tell me I'm a funny guy. I can trade pop culture references with an alien. Did you like the movie?"

"I thought it spoke to a fundamental problem of your species, Mr. Melamed."

"It's *Major* Melamed," he said a little too stiffly. "The fundamental problem with us? That's interesting. You don't think we're all a bunch of bloodthirsty serial killers, surely? Your command of English is excellent, and it's evident you've watched our broadcasts. We're not all Dr. Hannibal Lecter. That's a fundamental misunderstanding of humanity. Surprising mistake, given your other advances. But maybe you're full of surprising mistakes. Is that how you ended up here?"

The alien stepped closer to the screen, and Melamed fought the urge to step back.

"You misunderstand me," Cinnamon said. "I do not think you are all bloodthirsty killers. The fundamental flaw I refer to is your species' inability to combat problems. The character of Dr. Lecter escaped his prison to kill again repeatedly."

Melamed turned his back on the prisoner to retrieve the chair. He'd lost a point from the outset, and the break in the flow of the conversation gave him a moment to regain his composure and begin anew.

The heavy chair's metal feet scraped on the concrete as he dragged it close to the screen. Once seated, he looked up at the tall alien. He'd memorized the proposed questions on Colonel Fresco's list. She was in a hurry for answers, but his strategy was to establish some sort of rapport before cutting to the mission-critical questions.

"You've monitored our broadcasts for some time, I take it?"

"Decades, yes."

"Do you read English as well as you speak it?"

"Sadly, I do not read any of your many languages. The voice you are hearing is generated by a machine. I subvocalize in my language and the machine translates. With it, I can communicate in many human languages, though having so many strikes me as tediously inefficient. No wonder so few humans can come to common cause and cooperate with each other. Pardon the observation, but it is another fatal flaw of your kind."

Though it made him a little queasy, Melamed scanned the alien's body again. He could detect no devices and wondered if the translator was beneath the thing's armor or perhaps even implanted.

"The Hannibal Lecter reference is amusing, but the books are better than the movie. Too bad you are illiterate. If you could read, you might appreciate our good points."

"My translator does not decipher your symbolic representations, but in any event, Amazon does not deliver to the Marianas Trench."

Irony. Melamed had not expected humor from one of the monsters taking over the Earth. It was like finding out Hitler loved limericks and knock-knock jokes.

"Are you comfortable?" the major asked.

"Reasonably so, except for the lights. They are very bright."

"Your species doesn't like bright light?"

"We're also camera-shy. Recordings are an invasion of our privacy. Upon studying your media, one of our first horrors was to discover that you eat communally. We do not eat in front of each other."

Melamed shrugged. "Mostly we eat with our eyes glued to a screen and ignore each other. We like watching television, just like you."

The major turned back to one of the guards. "It is bright in here. Turn down the lights. Can you do fifty percent?"

Once the lights were dimmed, the alien thanked him and added, "We do appreciate courtesy."

"You know my name. What is yours?"

"You could not pronounce it properly without a translator. Your soldiers call me Cinnamon."

"Does that bother you?"

"A name is of little importance. The essence beneath the label is what matters. Your kind seems very invested in labels. That is not a value we share."

The major shrugged. "As you wish."

"There is an aspect of human behavior that puzzles me. May I ask you a question?"

"That could be interesting. I'll answer your questions if you answer mine."

"That could prove amusing."

Condescending prick, Melamed thought. "I'll go first. What are you and what is your fleet's objective?"

"Our race is the Mortchallin. We've come to make a home here and to do that, we will eliminate your species. I am not a soldier, but this will happen. My research of human actions is conclusive."

"I expected you to say you've come in peace."

"We have not."

"You don't want to be taken to our leader?"

"Your politicians are of little consequence. As you might say, the wheels are already in motion. Your idioms are fascinating. I don't understand them all, but I do appreciate that one. But no matter! To your question, you are doomed. Our ships are here to ensure your elimination transpires."

The alien's candor was shocking. The major was not optimistic by nature and had expected subterfuge. If the alien continued to be so forthright, he thought he might actually get actionable intelligence for Colonel Fresco after all.

"May I ask my question now?" Cinnamon asked.

The major motioned for him to go ahead.

"Please explain this motion." The alien shrugged its massive shoulders. "You've done it twice now, and I've seen no clear explanation for this element of your body language."

Melamed gave the alien a hard look. The stakes for the human race were life and death, but the thing seemed to be unconcerned for its fate. In his experience, prisoners always worried about their future. Cinnamon seemed remarkably unconcerned for itself. That carefree note rang an alarm bell. The aliens had superior technology. Perhaps a team of alien soldiers were on their way as he sat there. He didn't want to be put in a position of committing to hand-to-hand combat with a bunch of things that were part insect, part Komodo dragon, and part octopus.

The alien brought him out of his reverie. "Major Melamed? Do you know why you make that motion?"

"Shrugging? It can mean a couple of things. There's the helpless shrug, like, hey! Whaddayagonnado? It can also suggest you don't care, like, hey! Who cares?"

"Humans shrug often. Now I understand why. Thank you."

Drawn in, the major blurted, "Why's that?"

"I do not wish to be rude, but the gesture is appropriate since so many of you are helpless and careless."

"But you don't wish to be rude, huh? Bad news, then. That was rude."

"I apologize."

"Make it up to me." He thought of an easy question from the colonel's list. "One of your ships over New York attacked civilians.

Many were killed. We received one report that the ship broadcast a message before the attack. I'm very curious what that message would be. I don't suppose you know?"

"I do. It is part of the ritual to declare, *Chumagen Kintella*, followed by *Kintela Chumagen*. It means Begin the End and End the Beginning."

"Ritual?"

"Before the harvest. The Mortchallin are carnivores. You are meat. We honor the herd before the harvest."

"Oh."

"A nice change from consuming sea life."

"Wait, we're being invaded because you guys are tired of shopping in the seafood aisle?"

The first rule is that an interrogator should never seem surprised. Major Melamed was sweating through his shirt. Confronted by an unknown enemy with superior technology and no apparent remorse, the situation looked grim on the human side of the equation. By Melamed's calculations, the math was downright dire.

"Major?"

"Uh, yes?"

"I believe it is my turn to ask a question."

Melamed nodded.

"What does your name mean?"

"Excuse me?"

"In broadcasts of your fictions, I have noticed there is a sameness to many of the narratives. One exception I have observed is the variety in your names. Some names seem to be linked to the occupations of ancestors. Your name strikes me as unusual, for instance. I do not believe I have heard the name Boaz Melamed before."

"You probably wouldn't see it in the credits, either."

"Pardon my ignorance, but as I mentioned, I do not read your language."

"Right. Let's see. My mother named me Boaz. She liked it because it means strength. It's Hebrew, as is Melamed. That means teacher, so put it together and it means strong teacher."

"Do you teach in the military?"

"No, I talk to people. People like you."

"I am Mortchallin," the alien said. "I am not people."

"Aren't we all just people under the skin?"

"No. From what I have observed, your kind has an immense capacity for self-mythologizing. As someone who has traveled extensively, I must risk rudeness. I must inform you that you are not the center of the universe or even this galaxy." The alien paused, then pointed two of its arms up and to the right. "The center of this galaxy is far away in that direction."

"So we aren't all brothers and sisters, huh?"

"The difference between you and me is as great as the distance of my journey to arrive here before you."

The alien feels superior. Maybe I can use that. "Wouldn't it be wonderful to close that gap? Have you considered that? Perhaps you have it in you to be a strong teacher."

"I did agree to answer your questions."

Melamed sighed. "I took a class in art history once. In your studies of the human race, have you seen many of our paintings?"

"On PBS and several historical documentaries, yes."

"Something just struck me. In very old paintings of Jesus — sorry, do you know who I'm talking about?"

"Jesus Christ? Yes. Certain of your media talk of this figure extensively."

"Very old paintings depict his capture, his trial, and his execution. Christ is depicted in a way that suggests he's in control. His death and resurrection were predestined, and he's not surprised one bit. You remind me of those paintings. You're injured and you're a prisoner, yet you don't seem surprised. You hardly seem bothered."

"I know the future."

"Have you got a time machine, as well?"

"Not precisely, but a sequence of events has been set in motion. Our conquest of your planet is inevitable. It's already mostly complete."

Melamed's stomach churned. "You talk a lot of prideful shit for an alien whose ship crashed. How did that happen, anyway?"

"An error in judgment, an act of hubris, a surprising act of defiance. You are probing for weakness, but it was a mistake that will not be repeated. Your kind believe in luck. I find luck an absurd notion. Events occur or they do not. However, in your parlance, it was a long shot, a lucky shot."

"So you won't tell me?"

"I will. A flame brought by a human prisoner ignited the ship's atmosphere. I watched it happen. An atmosphere exchange sequencer malfunctioned and worked too slowly. The other ships were watching. Undoubtedly, repairs will have already been completed. There is no weakness there for you to report to your superiors, no ongoing failure to exploit."

"Why should I believe you, Cinnamon?"

"That is the first time you have called me that, Major. You believe on some level the name denigrates me. It does not. The Mortchallin have nothing to fear from you, so why would I lie?"

"Because we are enemies."

"Are you enemies with a cow or a pig, Major? Perhaps, as they are slaughtered they see you as an enemy. However, the butcher is just doing his or her job, are they not?"

Melamed stood up quickly from his chair and stepped closer. "You're smug. You said it was hubris that brought down your ship. We still might surprise you. We might not be cows easily taken to slaughter. Maybe we're wolves in the woods, ready to fight back."

"I'm sure you will fight back, Major. That is your nature."

"I'm a strong teacher, Cinnamon. I'm really hoping humans get a chance to teach you a lesson. What is your nature, Cinnamon? What's the meaning of your real name? Can you translate that?"

The alien tilted its head back and forth as if weighing its answer. "My kind do not ascribe meaning to our names. They only ease communications among individuals. We all work toward one common goal. It would be as if your name was 1234. Do you understand?"

Melamed sat again, mimicking the posture of an eager pupil. "Teach me. You're so wise and advanced, so above it all. Why don't you let us live instead of committing genocide? Wouldn't that be the enlightened thing to do?"

"And keep you as what? Pets? That would not honor you. We desire sustenance, not your subjugation. The desire for power over another is a human trait. Please understand, this is not personal."

"You're talking about killing us all, so it is very personal."

"No more so than the farmer who takes the hen's eggs or the rancher who cuts the cow's throat."

"What if we were to offer you our cattle, instead?"

"You wish to renounce your genocide of a less intelligent species to save your own? Do you not see the irony? You can't very well call us cruel given all you do to animals when you could be eating plants. You are omnivorous. We are carnivores."

"For a peaceful solution, why not try it? What if all of the Western world went vegan tomorrow? Would that spare us your wrath?"

"Major, you know the stakeholders would never agree to such an arrangement. We have observed humans for a long time. Selflessness is a virtue espoused by a majority and practiced by a minority. The Mortchallin understand sacrifice for the collective. Sacrifice is often shunned by humans. Your heroic martyrs stand out because there are so few of them."

Melamed ran his fingers through his hair and loosened his tie. With his head in his hands, he stared at the floor. "What about virtue? Does anyone in your fleet have any? Do you believe in anything? Do you have a god that tells you what you're doing is wrong?"

"You have many gods here. Do you follow their edicts?"

The major shot back, "Since you believe you're so much better than us, I thought maybe you'd reach for higher heights. Do you believe in a higher power?"

"Belief? The Mortchallin do not believe things, Major. Either a thing is or it is not. Either our species benefits from an act or we do not. You asked me to teach you so learn this. You don't believe in the dawn of the sun each day. You can see the evidence of it. That is not a belief. That is a fact. Soon you will not be able to see the sun. That is not something I believe. That is a fact I know."

"So your kind has no compassion, and you don't cherish anything but cold facts, huh?"

The alien stared at him with those big yellow eyes. Coldness invaded Melamed's heart, and he had to look away.

When the alien spoke again, the words came slower than before, each syllable falling like a hammer blow. "There is one word that does signify something larger. Mortchallin is one of the few words in our language that is ... metaphoric. Mortchallin means Keepers of the Flame." The alien pointed to its thorax with one of its arms, circling the central plating of its armor. "The flame is the life of our species. We carry our flame to distant planets that are habitable or can be made habitable. That is how our kind survives. Farming your kind, we will survive. Your destruction is inevitable, but we do thank you for your cooperation."

"What about your destruction, Cinnamon? Are you worried at all about that? I've got a doctor here from New York. The Mortchallin killed a lot of people there, so he probably wouldn't mind vivisecting you without anesthesia."

"My individual death is of little consequence. Many more of our kind are coming."

Melamed paced back and forth, slowed his breathing, and focused on his list of questions. Colonel Fresco had brought him in for his experience, but his expertise hardly seemed relevant. He was as lost as the doctor who scoffed at trying to measure an alien's blood pressure.

The major had interviewed enemy combatants who were almost as smug as the alien. However, those prisoners were either delusional or trying to conceal their fear. The alien seemed so confident, it didn't mind answering his questions. At that, he decided to come at Cinnamon straight.

"What's already in motion that makes you so confident you will win this war?"

"We attacked and weakened you."

"And?"

"You will not be able to stop yourselves from escalating the conflict. Humans never learn the lesson. Your own narratives consistently suggest you are the authors of your own destruction. Self-destruction is your nature."

"Yeah, I've seen old reruns of *Gilligan's Island*, too. They never got off the island because of one idiot."

"For our plan to succeed, we don't need many idiots. Those in charge or who hold sway will do."

Melamed persisted. "We can be sneaky. We're survivors, too, top of our earthly food chain. Your ship got blown up because you underestimated us. You're doing that again right now, you smug bastard."

The alien moved for the first time, turning to one side. "It seems you have lost the thread of our agreement. This is no longer question and answer. That was rude. I suggest we wait until tomorrow at this time and see who was correct in their estimations of strengths and weaknesses. You're upset. We shouldn't speak anymore. Turn the bright lights back on if you wish. A futile attempt to punish me is in your nature."

Melamed's mouth went dry. He had been about to give the order to bring the lights back up to full strength. The alien had robbed him of his one meager weapon.

The major straightened his tie and grabbed his hat. He was halfway to the exit when the alien called after him.

"Major Melamed? I feel I have been unkind. It is not your fault you do not understand. The Mortchallin value truth but that doesn't mean we lack compassion. It may not appear so, but I have found many of your fictional broadcasts charming. We ... *I* appreciate you."

"So? Does that mean you'd consider peace talks? To work out a bargain we could find — "

"You misunderstand. I only wanted to convey that we chose this course of action because humans are doomed anyway. We dislike wasting resources. Our way, your deaths will serve a noble purpose: our survival."

"Wait! What?"

"Humans were chosen for the slaughter because of your lack of viability. We have been patient in our evaluations, so perhaps the truth of your fate will be of some comfort. If we failed to destroy you, you would soon end yourselves. We will be quick and merciful. A life without mercy is rude, and as I said, we do not care for rudeness."

At that, the alien turned away.

The major's heart pounded. All Melamed could hear was his pulse pounding in his ears. He headed out the door at a trot. By the time he arrived at Colonel Fresco's office, he was panting and sweaty.

Fresco was on her phone. She hung up and looked at him sharply. "I've been watching the camera feed. You got nothing. Are you going to let that thing stew for a while before going back in? Or do you plan to take that bet and see if the sun comes up day after tomorrow?"

"I got everything I could."

She grabbed a pen and a blank sheet of paper. "Stand and deliver, Major. What did I miss?"

"The alien said it all. We are the authors of our own destruction."

"Speak plainly."

"The Mortchallin easily destroyed any resistance on the ground and in the air. What's left of our capacity to counterattack?"

"Just what was shielded by mountains of dirt and concrete, Major."

"Or what was deep underwater. Our subs."

"I feel a migraine coming on, Melamed."

"Nukes! They left us the nukes! We've got 5,600 nukes, and they're damn sure we're going to use them to counterattack. That's what they want. The nuclear flash will be bright, but once the party's over, Earth will be a wreck. Lots of smoke and clouds. They prefer dim light. I believe the atmosphere will be affected sufficiently that Earth will become more hospitable to the aliens."

Colonel Fresco put down her pen. The page before her remained blank. She sat back in her chair and rubbed her temples. "Well, that's that then."

"What do you mean?"

"The nuclear triad is our last line of defense against the global threat of an invasion by a superior hostile force. The Air Force and all our surface naval fleet are knocked out, but the submarine fleet is at DEFCON 3. We're fifteen minutes from the counterattack at all times."

Melamed glanced at his watch. *Fifteen minutes. Could be fifteen minutes to going nuclear. It might have already happened! Or maybe it'll happen in half an hour or tomorrow when the president is through waffling.*

"Missile silos across the world are already primed and waiting for the final order," Colonel Fresco said.

Melamed's legs felt like jelly. He sat in the chair opposite his CO. His skin suddenly felt too tight and his chest too small for his pounding heart. "If we fire nuclear weapons, we'll be giving them what they want. We'll be destroying the planet, and they will feed on our corpses like ... like Komodo dragons."

Hardly blinking, Fresco stared back at him and said nothing.

"Is the alien right?" he asked. "Are we really going to? I mean — "

"If we don't, every other nation with nuclear capability will attack."

"So let them."

"The world looks to us to lead. We'll look weak if we do nothing, and we *must* do something."

"Must? Even if it's the wrong thing?"

"Israel, France, and Russia say they already tried conventional weapons to no effect. People are howling for blood. I'm told the president is listening to the loudest and angriest voices in the situation room."

The idiots in charge and those who hold sway over them, Melamed thought. The alien was so confident in how the sequence of events would unfold that Cinnamon had as much as warned him.

"The answer can't be to do as the enemy expects, to die exactly as they expect. We can't cater to the lowest common denominator!"

"We've done it before," Fresco said coolly.

"But we have to prove the invaders wrong! This feels like a science teacher bending over backward to agree with the dumbest kid in class."

"Not new," she replied. "In fact, that happens every day everywhere. That will be all, Major."

"But, Colonel! If we are to avoid becoming the authors of our own destruction, we have to defy our first and worst impulses!"

"You understand, even if I agree with you, it's not up to me. Of course, I will pass the intel up the chain of command with my strongest recommendations to hold off. However, with nothing but nukes with which to respond — "

"The order can't be stopped?"

"It could, but I have to agree with the alien. Under the circumstances, exercising the nuclear option is inevitable."

"But — "

"I'm not arguing this with you. I concede you're probably right, Major, but I will be asked if I think the alien is lying. I can only say I have a ninety-five percent certainty that firing nukes will play into their creepy many-fingered hands. A lack of other options, pride, and five percent doubt will be enough for the Commander in Chief to give the order."

Melamed sagged in his chair, his eyes wet. Colonel Fresco watched him a moment and gave an eloquent shrug.

IV

No one can know the inner workings of another's mind.
Not even among those nearest and dearest.

THE LAST SUPPER

On the outskirts of Leadville, Colorado, Kurt David tossed another log on the fire. Once on a Labor Day long weekend thirty-four years previously, he'd dug this fire pit with his brother Dale. They lined its walls with concrete blocks and topped it with smooth stones from the nearby Arkansas River. Esophageal cancer had taken Dale in '98, but Kurt and the fire pit remained.

He'd rarely used their creation, but with the power out, Kurt was thankful for it. He gave his dead brother a silent nod for the fire pit he hadn't wanted. Dale had been trying to kick the booze that summer and needed a project. Kurt's brother didn't kick alcohol, only dodged it a while. Still, that warm September weekend working on this pit with his little brother was one of their best times together.

Grease dripped from the two chickens on the spit and sizzled, feeding flashes of flame. Rekindling old memories of Dale and staring into the fire, Kurt did not hear Judy arrive by his side. He gave his wife a warm smile. "Just another few minutes. Good thing we don't have one of those fancy electric testers. An old-fashioned thermometer will do us just fine."

Clad in her heaviest sweater, Judy crossed her arms tightly to her chest, "Wouldn't want to die of food poisoning. That would be ironic."

"And miss the end of the world? Can't have that."

Judy winced. "It might not be the end. People are wrong about things all the time."

"Luke seems awfully sure."

"He was always the most excitable." Judy tried to sound breezy, but her eyes were wet. She'd always been the kind to cry in secret and put on a brave face.

"If he weren't sure, Luke wouldn't be here," Kurt said. "He wouldn't be so drunk, either."

Kurt cast a glance back toward the house. Candles provided the only illumination. He couldn't see his son, but he imagined him standing in the living room, watching his old man cook. Luke had arrived drunk and brought two bottles of wine with him. His son had claimed the alcohol was for his parents to soften the blow. It seemed to Kurt it was Luke who sought comfort from the gifts he'd brought.

The men of the David family had a weakness for alcohol. Kurt had never kept any booze in the house for fear it would dull his wits. He'd refrained from chastising his son, though. Tonight was not a night for enforcing discipline.

Tonight is for what, though? When encountering a situation you've never faced before and doom looms, don't judge yourself too harshly on what bubbles up on its own.

If Luke's information was correct, there would be no one to eulogize them. All that was left was to be kind to each other and try to remember the good times.

When the future gets short, and the present is flying by too fast, it's natural to look to the past. We dwell in memories because those events are far away from what's soon to come.

Kurt searched for something happy from better times and soon let out a low chuckle.

"Something funny?" Judy asked. "If you have a joke, I need to hear it."

"No joke, Judy. That's what my mother called you behind your back. No Joke Judy. It's time you finally found out and I confessed. Mom thought you were a sourpuss."

"Really?"

"No." But it *was* true. Kurt's mother never cared much for her daughter-in-law.

No Joke Judy doesn't need to know that truth, Kurt thought. *And I wish Luke hadn't come all this way just to tell us we're going to die horribly, probably tomorrow.*

Judy swatted her husband's shoulder and turned to go back inside. She called over her shoulder, "Pay attention to the meat and turn that spit. You burn it, you eat it!"

"Yes, dear. You know, you are pretty serious!" Kurt replied.

Before she shut the front door behind her, she called back, "How do I explain? Oh, yeah! Shut it, old man!"

With his wife safely out of earshot, Kurt added, "But it's a serious night, isn't it? Can't shake it. It's a grim night. I might have cereal and eggs and bacon for breakfast, but tonight is the funeral feast. Might not be alive by lunch."

Kurt's low back ached as he bent to turn the spit, but he enjoyed the smell of the cooking meat. If the power weren't out and if Luke hadn't arrived with his news, it would have been a pleasant evening.

A lot of people are thinking about what would have been tonight. Kurt pushed that idea away. No need to be morbid. Maybe tomorrow, after breakfast, would be a better time to dwell on his demise.

"Try to enjoy the now," he told himself. "You've always enjoyed power outages when they were brief."

When he and Judy were young, a night without power was an opportunity for passion. "May as well," he'd tell her. "With the power out, what else is there to do? Can't watch TV, so let's do each other."

As the years wore on and time wore them down, they talked more when the lights went out. Darkness drained away distractions and memories thought to be lost sometimes resurfaced.

Kurt tried to put on a brave face to match the strength of Judy's denialism, but he believed his son's earnest report of the alien invasion. *Soon, we'll be nothing more than memories in the brains of our murderers.*

When his father lay on his deathbed, Kurt holding one hand and Dale the other, James David was loopy on painkillers. Still, he had uttered one gem. "Old men shouldn't be morbid. We're so close to death all the time anyway, gettin' all ghoulish about it could become a full-time occupation. Be wary of that when your turn comes, boys. The end is still plenty far off for you, and I'm glad of that. If I'm being honest, I resent you for your youth."

"There it is," Kurt muttered. "A memory I thought dead, resurrected."

Kurt looked southwest toward the outline of Mount Massive. After Dale died, Kurt had found new urgency in staying healthy. For several years after burying his brother, he committed to walking daily at a brisk pace. He didn't tell anyone he was training his body. That would sound silly. However, a couple of times a year, if the weather was fine enough, he would take two days to climb the mountain and hike the three-mile summit ridge.

It was a proven way to stay in shape. The summer before Luke went to boot camp, he quit his job as an usher at the Tabor Opera House. Luke hiked that same mountain through the summer, increasing the weight in his pack until the straps made his shoulders red and raw. He got so strong that by September, he was more than ready for the physical challenges the Air Force threw at him. After their first long run, Luke was made leader of his squad.

Kurt remembered how sunny and warm it was the day he and Judy dropped Luke off at the bus. As they watched him go, Judy rubbed her husband's arm. "He's doing this because of you, you know."

"I don't see it. I'm an engineer more than anything."

"For the military."

"Tangentially. If anything, he's following your lead. If he wanted to follow in my footsteps, he would have gone to Cornell."

"What? *That* safety school?" Judy teased. She had attended Vassar and Brown. In her eyes, there were no other educational institutions, just pretenders to the crown.

Judy had studied computer science at Brown. Kurt met her at a research conference in Chicago. His focus was artificial intelligence. She programmed navigation software for drones. They were only together in Chicago for one week, but that proved enough time to conceive Dara. Luke's older sister brought them together. They married in Dillon, Colorado, and Dara was born five months later.

Kurt's mom told everyone our beautiful baby girl was the biggest preemie that Judy's doctor had ever seen. His chuckle at that memory was soon suffocated by the thought of Dara. She didn't know what was coming. She lived in Towson, a suburb of Baltimore. There was no way to say goodbye.

Kurt knuckled a tear from his eye. Their brilliant daughter had become a senior analyst for a charity he didn't fully grasp. The charity had something to do with providing aid to refugees around the world, but Dara's expertise demanded deep dives into meteorological data.

Dara rarely expressed interest in his work and only spoke vaguely of her own. She had always belonged to Judy and Luke was born a daddy's boy. Until this night, that had never seemed a problem.

At that moment, Dara was probably sitting in the dark waiting for the lights to pop back on. She would have no idea of the malevolent forces that had arrived on Earth.

I envy her that ignorance, he thought. *I resent her peace of mind.*

"Dad?"

Luke held two wine glasses in his hand. He offered one, but Kurt shook his head. "No, thanks. I gotta keep turning the spit. I'm pleased to see you've switched to using a glass. You were drinking out of a bottle when you arrived."

"C'mon, Dad. If not now, when?"

Kurt let out a guffaw. "No time left to become a proper alcoholic, huh?"

"Something like that."

"I was just thinking about you running up and down Mount

Massive with that heavy pack. The last summer you lived at home, I mean."

Luke looked to the mountain. "I always thought that was a silly name."

"What? Mount Massive. Why? Too linear?"

"Too much like they asked a stupid kid what to name the mountain. Sounds like a villain's fortress out of a comic book."

Kurt nodded in agreement and checked the birds with a meat thermometer. Peering at it in the firelight, he couldn't quite make out the numbers on the gauge. He offered it to his son. "Can't read it. That okay?"

Luke bobbed his head. "Perfect. What's the matter? Forget your reading glasses?"

"In better light, I'm fine." A sliver of defensiveness entered his tone which he immediately regretted. Luke had a knack for pushing his buttons, and tonight was not the night for arguments. "I don't drive at night anymore. When it gets dark, it's too dark for me to drive and when headlights are coming at me, it's too damn bright. Getting old is — "

"Something I might not get to do," Luke said.

Tonight is not about conquerors from the stars, the old man thought. *Tonight is about us, about family. If Jesus hadn't been so accusatory at the last supper, maybe Judas would have loved him enough to tell the Romans to go screw themselves.*

Kurt cleared his throat. "I like a fire, but let's get inside and have a feast. It's kind of like our old camp back in the woods. You ran around with your pellet gun, remember? Each night we'd roast hotdogs, pop popcorn, and burn marshmallows."

"S'mores, Dad. You're thinking of s'mores."

"Am I?"

"Maybe you did that stuff with Dara. I came along a lot later. I remember the pellet gun, but I only went up to that camp once, maybe twice. Dara was always your favorite — "

"You think so? Everyone thinks somebody else is the favorite."

"Whatever, just try not to confuse us. She's the one who can grow a thicker mustache."

Kurt said nothing in reply. With some difficulty, he lifted the skewer that held the two cooked chickens and placed them on a silver platter. "I think we got that platter from someone when we got married. I can't remember the last time we used it."

"Christmases and Thanksgiving," Luke said. "Special occasions only."

Both father and son looked skyward warily. After a long moment, Kurt muttered, "As you say, if not now, when?"

Judy had set the table as if it were Christmas. The napkins were red and green. She'd pulled out their finest silverware. "I never use the good eatin' irons enough, do I?"

Luke gave her a look. "Eating irons?"

"That's what my father used to call them," Judy explained. "He was from Maine, so he always thought he was funny."

Kurt added, "Your father joked about never approving of me, but it was never really a joke. He just thought he was being subtle."

Judy tilted her head back and forth, weighing her options. "This is where I'm supposed to rise to my long-suffering husband's defense, but I could have married better."

"And I could have married more women," Kurt parried.

Despite their attempt at banter to lighten the mood, their son remained morose. Luke plopped himself down at the dining room table and smeared a big dollop of peanut butter on a slab of sourdough bread.

"We had a few potatoes and lots of carrots left. I should have cooked up some to go with the chicken."

"This is fine," Luke said. "We can break the rules. Rules don't matter much anymore. I've been making my bed every morning for years as if someone was still inspecting my quarters. What a waste of time all that was."

As Kurt carved the chicken, he kept glancing at his son. He wanted to say something to ease Luke's mind, but no words of solace came. The truth was, he wanted to tell Luke to stop drinking or at least slow down. His father and brother had both been sloppy drunks. Kurt hated trying to have a conversation with a drunk.

"So?" Kurt asked finally. "Should we pack a bag of chicken and peanut butter sandwiches for the road? Are the MPs going to show up any minute to drag you back to base?"

"That won't be a problem, Dad."

"Going AWOL is a serious thing."

"Not in this case, it's not." Luke drained his wine glass and refilled it immediately, as much as the glass could hold.

"Get some food in you before you finish the next one, son. This is not a race. Pace yourself and the buzz will last longer."

Luke let out a low curse. "It *is* a race, Dad. We don't have much time."

Kurt glanced at his wife. Staring at her empty plate, Judy said, "Peanut butter and chicken. That's kind of a Thai restaurant thing, isn't it? You know, I've had Chinese food, but have we ever had Thai, Kurt?"

"Those little spring rolls with plum sauce, I think. That's it, isn't it?"

"We should have done more," Luke said.

Neither of his parents thought he was speaking of spring rolls.

Kurt used tongs to put the chicken pieces in two big bowls. He offered to serve Judy, but she shook her head. "Not hungry just now, love. You go ahead."

"You always lost your appetite under stress."

"And you always ate too much comfort food. Nobody needs that much comfort. I should have given you teddy bears to cuddle instead of cooking for you all these years. You'd be thinner."

Kurt grinned. "Now, now, let's keep it friendly." He served himself and passed the tongs to Luke. His son managed to place one drumstick on his plate, but he almost fumbled it.

Too drunk, Kurt thought. *Dale would have said he was "half in the bag." Or, "had a snootful."*

Luke seemed more interested in making another peanut butter sandwich anyway. "Peanut butter. I always thought of it as one word, but it's two, isn't it? It's butter, but it's made of peanuts. It's like when people talk about celebrities, we always think of them in terms of their first and last names. It's hard to imagine anyone calling a star by their first name. Tom Cruise was Tom Cruise or at least Mr. Cruise. How many people would have called him Tom?"

"*Was* Tom Cruise?" Judy sounded irritated. "The world's not over yet, is it?"

Luke froze for a moment. "Well ... the last report I saw, Los Angeles was gone. I assume he lived there."

"Gone?" Judy went white.

"Sorry, I shouldn't have said anything."

Judy cleared her throat. "Actually, I think I *do* want to know exactly what is going on."

"I don't know everything, Mom. Just scattered reports."

When Judy looked up from her plate, her tears glistened in the candlelight. "Is it possible this is all a drill? An exercise? Maybe even some elaborate hoax to see how many of you would desert?"

Luke stopped chewing and stared at his mother as if she'd just confessed to planting a bomb under his seat.

"The government has been hyping UFOs for years," Judy pressed. "Space Force, space tourism, going to Mars...it's all a bunch of nonsense to persuade us to spend tax money on useless toys for defense contractors. Your father and I ought to know. We were part of that machine. It's how we bought this house, for God's sake!"

Luke put down his knife. He looked sober. "Mom, I assure you, it's real. I got it from a buddy in Communications at Peterson. When we figured out there was nothing we could do, a friend at NORAD gave us a bus from the depths of the mountain. It was shielded from the EMP. If not for that, I couldn't have gotten here to say goodbye. I'd still be at Peterson wishing I was home. You're very lucky my boys dropped me off on their way. That's all there is to it. This invasion is happening, and nothing's gonna wish it away."

Judy stared at her son. The room got so quiet, Kurt felt he was making too much noise as he chewed.

"Tell us everything," Judy said. "No short shrift this time."

Luke took another long swallow of wine.

Soon, he'll have polished off all the booze he brought, Kurt thought. *Then maybe he can get back to being my son and stop reminding me of my brother.*

Luke repeated his story, much as he had before. He'd been in a hangar greasing an engine when the lights went out. "We've got backup power for emergencies. When a crisis hits or a war breaks out, we're one of the destinations for Air Force One. It's not like the power can go out at Peterson Space Force Base."

The new name still sounded strange to Kurt's ears. When he worked for the government, it had always been Peterson Air Force Base. The name change was serious and real, but like Massive Mountain, it sounded a bit silly.

"But the power didn't come back on?" Judy prompted.

"Not right away. Some genius figured a workaround. They managed to do something with the generators and the radios. As soon as the comms were back up, we started getting reports, mostly from civvies with ham radios. Most of the signals were so weak, their voices sounded like a fly in a bottle."

Judy was not satisfied. "And that's how you know LA is destroyed?"

"Yes."

"But how exactly?"

"The guy who saw it was up in the hills. He said it was a bright flash."

"Like a nuclear strike?" Kurt asked.

"The guy said it was more like something you'd see in a sci-fi movie. He described it as an energy weapon."

Judy leaned forward in her seat, eager to find any reason to believe the end was not near. "And that report sounded credible and from a trustworthy source?"

"Combined with all the other reports we got from around the world, yeah, I guess so. The brass believed it."

Kurt struck the table with his fist a little harder than he'd intended. "We bought this house over thirty years ago! Can you believe it? I can't believe it, and I live here! At first, we thought it would be an investment property, and we'd live in Colorado Springs full-time. But you know what I love about Leadville? It's such a small town, but it has such a colorful history. The Unsinkable Molly Brown! Guggenheim!"

"Dad, we're trying to — "

"C'mon, you two! It's amazing. Doc Holliday lived here shortly after the gunfight at the OK Corral!"

"And got away with shooting a policeman here," his wife replied. "What is it with old men and history? I caught him watching World War II documentaries, Luke. Last week, your father went on for twenty minutes about the invasion of Normandy."

"Fifteen minutes," Kurt grumbled. "I did stop when your eyes glazed over. I know that look you have."

"You're not as sensitive to my moods as you think you are. My eyes glazed over right away."

Kurt harpooned a chicken breast, but he couldn't help himself. He'd barely swallowed before he spoke again, "Maybe old fellas like me are fascinated with history because there's more behind us than there is ahead. We've seen a chunk of the arc of history — "

"Dad! Dad! Stop! There is no future! The arc of history ends with a steep drop to nothing! Who cares what came before? By this time tomorrow night, it's all going to be wiped away."

To Kurt, their last meal together suddenly tasted like dirt. The table looked so pretty and the candlelight warmed the room, but his skin went cold and clammy. He felt as if he'd swallowed a ball of lead.

"I'm sorry," Kurt said. "It seems ... I don't know what it seems. I just want to pretend, I guess. I'm not ready for everything to go away. *I'm* not ready to go away."

"Do you think any of us are?" Luke asked.

"No, of course ... no."

Judy reached out and patted her husband's hand. "You'll have to excuse us, Luke. It's our first end of the world scenario. What are the rules?"

"Sure," Kurt said. "Finish your story. Give it to us straight, Doc."

"A few will survive, but neither of you will make it," Luke said. "I'm sorry, but even if you were to survive by some miracle, the drugstore in town won't be carrying insulin anymore, Mom. And Dad, blood pressure medication will be hard to come by. It's going to get ugly fast."

"Another bit of history," Kurt said. "Nikita Khrushchev speaking on nuclear war said the living would envy the dead."

Judy squeezed his hand and said, "Dear? I love you. Please shut up."

"Okay."

She turned back to her son. "What aren't you telling us?"

"I'm going back," Luke said. "This has to be nothing more than a brief visit. I have to be back at Peterson by 1300 hours. My friends will be back at dawn to pick me up."

Startled, Kurt replied, "I thought you'd stay with us to watch the big show! Grand finale and all that!"

Judy slid a censorious glance at her husband and Kurt bobbed his head. "Shutting up again. Sorry."

"I've got to get back," Luke said. "Don't ask why, Mom. Just know that I do."

Kurt got up from the table. "I have to go check on the fire. Before you go, let's burn some marshmallows or something."

When he left them at the table, both wife and son were crying. He didn't want them to see his tears.

Standing at the edge of the fire pit, he looked to the stars. He didn't believe in God, but he thought how nice it would be if another, more benevolent alien race suddenly appeared to save the day and eliminate these locusts.

He forgot where he'd heard it, but someone once said nothing is impossible, but a lot of things are incredibly improbable. Enemies of these invaders showing up now seemed to be in the latter category. The galaxy was too vast and too accustomed to injustice for that.

On the day Dale died in his hospital bed, his brother looked so much like their father, Kurt found his appearance haunting. Gray and weak, Dale couldn't swallow anymore and used a suction device to get rid of the extra saliva.

A chaplain had appeared in the doorway to ask if Dale would find comfort in prayer. His brother's voice was weak, but his resolve remained strong. "Reverend, I drank myself to death out of sadness at the only eternal truth I know. Whatever power may be hiding out there in the universe, it does not give a single shit about me. I'm not going to start trying to kiss any divine ass at this late date. If there is a God, I fear he'd lose respect for me if I weakened at the eleventh hour."

Like most people, Kurt had assumed he himself would collapse from a heart attack or a stroke at home. That was his ideal. The second choice was a long slow decline that might put him in the same hospital room as his late brother.

"Dale? If you're listening, I admire your bravery at the end. I'm not feeling very brave, but then again, I don't think I'm going to wind up in a hospital bed getting massages from pretty nurses, either. It seems my choices are to die via energy weapon or maybe starvation while the rest of the country falls to alien invaders. Did not have that on my bingo card."

Luke's voice startled him. "There is another, kinder option, Dad."

"Hey, again. Didn't see you coming. My hearing must be going. How's your mom doing?"

"She went to take a nap. She wants to stay up all night, but to do that, she needs some rest."

"Good on her if she can do it. What if they attack right away and she dies in her sleep? Wouldn't want to miss the end of the world."

Luke shook his head. "Not funny, but good for you for trying. I have to tell you a couple of things."

"You just told us we're doomed, so I assume the news gets cheerier from here on out."

"I don't grease engines for a living, Dad. I told you I knew a guy in Comms. I'm the guy in Comms. I'm an Intelligence officer. I'm going back to the mountain. My CO knew you didn't live far away, so he told me and a couple others to go and get back in time for the fireworks."

"NORAD's going to let you in the doomsday ark?"

Luke nodded.

"Congratulations, son. I'm happy for you." But he felt no happiness for Luke. It was the right thing to say, but he resented being left behind.

Once upon a time, I wasn't so disposable, Kurt thought. *Of course, that was back in a lost time when people still studied Latin in school. I was a child prodigy, a math whiz. I knew how to use a slide rule like a calculator.* He hadn't actually been old enough to use it for that, but he'd known how.

Kurt stared into the dying fire. "I'm surprised you could come out to see us off. So? What's going to happen?"

Luke took a long time to answer. Finally, he said, "Authorized personnel will go down into the mountain and lock the door behind us."

"Please don't talk to me like I'm a very old man or a very young child."

"The plan is to nuke the monsters. We're coordinating with other nuclear powers for one lethal strike. When it happens, it's supposed to come all at once."

Kurt let out a harrumph. "Finally, on *this*, everyone cooperates."

Luke nodded. "Against a common enemy, we are finally united."

"With nukes? I've heard this story before. We have to destroy the village to save it?"

Luke shifted back and forth on the balls of his feet. "If we don't do something, they're going to wipe us out, Dad. The aliens are the new apex predators."

"We have been awfully comfortable at the top of the food chain for a while," Kurt conceded.

"Try to think of it this way, Dad. We're doing this because we have hope. We have reason to hope the nukes will work."

Kurt turned to stare at his son in the cast of the guttering flames. He couldn't believe he and his beautiful, brilliant wife could have produced a child so stupid. "Let's hear it. I won't tell anyone."

"We captured one of them. The prisoner told us things. There was a great debate whether to believe the intelligence. The alien may as well have been daring us to go nuclear on their asses."

Kurt wiped his forehead with his palm. His hand came away wet with sweat. "You're telling me the aliens used reverse psychology on our best and brightest?"

"Well, no, not our best and brightest. I'm talking about the politicians making the decisions."

"So they think nukes will do the job? Kill the invasion force?"

"Top people examined the wreckage. Our experts think nukes will do the necessary damage."

"Shouldn't they test that theory on one spaceship first?"

"And lose the element of surprise? You're stuck in the gap between military strategy and scientific thinking."

"Sounds like the difference between recklessness and logic," Kurt said. "But no one ever listened to me. That's why I was so relieved to retire from government service."

Luke stepped closer and put a hand on his father's shoulder. "The thinking is that once the nukes fly, we'll wait it out and begin again. We have personnel filling up bunkers right now."

"And you'll be one of them. Is this some grand adventure to you, son? We gave you a biblical name, but maybe we should have called you Adam. Do you already have your eye on an Eve at NORAD? Somebody with whom you can repopulate the Earth in a few years?"

"This is an adventure, Dad. We've got supplies to last for years. Some of the greatest minds the world has to offer are being gathered up."

That didn't sound like his son. Kurt was almost certain he was quoting from a speech he'd heard from one of the architects of this mad scheme.

"They're calling it the Great Reset," Luke continued. "It's been talked about for years, but this is the real thing."

Suddenly exhausted and not trusting his sore back, Kurt sat at the edge of the fire pit. The fire had died down considerably, but the embers still radiated enough heat that his back felt better.

"So," Kurt said, "this is happening."

"Like it or not."

"And? If the nukes don't destroy these new conquistadors?"

"Then, when the radiation dies down, and the world is a little more habitable, we'll sneak out of our holes and kill them all later. With enough patience and ingenuity, insurgencies always win out over an occupying force. You like history. You have to admit that's true."

Kurt's chin sank to his chest. He could barely look at his son. "Any helpful examples you could draw from history don't feature a species from outer space with technology beyond our imagination. What do the aliens look like, anyway?"

"Monsters, just monsters. The report I heard described them as a mix between a squid and an insect. They prefer to breathe methane. As soon as I heard that, I thought they must stink like farts! Turns out they smell like cinnamon."

"Methane is odorless," Kurt replied. "For safety, they add something to natural gas to make it smell like rotten eggs so people know to run from a leak."

"Of course, *you'd* know that."

Kurt shrugged. "I used to think I knew a lot of things. I'm not so sure anymore."

Luke sat beside his father and put an arm around his shoulders. Kurt felt so small then. Somehow, enough years had passed that they were switching roles. Now Luke was the dispenser of hard truths about how the world failed to work. Kurt was the naive child railing against injustices he could not accept.

"Oscar Wilde came to Leadville once. Did you know that?"

"If I did, I forgot about it," Luke admitted.

"He came out here to the sticks to hold forth to a bunch of regular people, criminals, and rubes. His aim was to convince them of the virtue of the Aesthetic Movement. Any idea what that was? You should know this. It happened at the theater you used to work at."

Luke took a deep breath in and let out a long sigh. "I'm sure you're going to tell me all about it."

"I get it. I'm an old windbag. This is our last go-round, so indulge your beloved father for just a second, will you? The idea behind the Aesthetic Movement was simply to do art for art's sake. Wilde told everybody they should live life to the fullest. The only virtue in art was its own beauty. A bunch of locals planned to come to his presentation to mock him. Fortunately, that didn't happen, but what's interesting is that Oscar Wilde came here to try to elevate people. Agree with him or not, there's a bit of a contradiction to his message. Slogging out to the sticks probably wasn't old Oscar's idea of living life to the fullest."

"My ride is coming back at dawn, Dad. Get to your point."

"Two things. First, Wilde was trying to tell people that art should be beautiful, never sentimental. And above all, don't bother trying to teach anybody anything. Just shut up and enjoy it."

Luke nodded. "And the second thing?"

"He was right. Don't try to teach anybody anything, at least not anybody in power. It's apparent from what you just told me that they're too stupid to learn."

To his credit, Luke had the grace to laugh.

Kurt laughed, too, but bitterly. "You told your mother everyone's going to die, but you don't think you will."

"There's a chance I will, but I've got better odds than most. I have the resources of the US military behind me."

"You're not a general, son. You're the shield and the fodder. You're one of the guys they use to stay safe."

"I'm confident in our leadership. Not the politicians, but my immediate chain of command."

That's the problem with idiots, Kurt thought. *They don't know enough to suffer crippling anxiety and doubt.*

He wanted to tell Luke the truth as he saw it. Instead, he gave in to the inevitability of the apocalypse. "I love you, son."

"I love you, too, Dad. I'm sorry I can't take you and Mom into the mountain with me."

Kurt considered that a sweet and easy sentiment, but he doubted its veracity. Luke pictured himself as the hero in a big action flick. Having his elderly parents along for the ride didn't fit that narrative.

"I'd just cramp your style," Kurt said.

Luke took a few deep breaths and squeezed his father's shoulder tighter. Despite the sour smell of his son's breath, he leaned in.

I used to carry you, Kurt thought. *First in my arms and then on my shoulders. And now here we are. Youth's progression and age's deterioration are always the same, but somehow a surprise every time.*

"Unfortunately, there's more, Dad. The cities the aliens attack, they don't seem to have a hierarchy or logic to their targets. Wherever there are humans, that's a target."

"They don't recognize borders, and we're all the same to them, huh? That's something else we should have learned. Every astronaut that looked out over the Earth from orbit saw us as one thing, one system. I always thought that was a good message."

"Dad?"

"Yeah, still here."

"A report I saw said they hit Baltimore hard. Dara's already gone."

Kurt leaned forward and put his head in his hands. Dead? How could this be? He said nothing. All he could do was gasp for air and weep quietly.

When he could get his breath again, Kurt begged his son not to tell his mother. "I won't."

Kurt knuckled the tears away. Somehow, he'd have to keep this secret from Judy. Sharing the weight of his grief would be selfish.

He slowed his breathing and turned to Luke. "Why did you tell me? You didn't have to tell me any of this. You surely didn't have to come home to tell me your sister's dead. We could have gone to the end, happy and ignorant."

Luke stood suddenly. "Coming here was a risk, but I thought I owed you both. I didn't want to tell you, but the truth is, I've never thought of you as a particularly strong person."

"No?" Kurt stared at his son wondering if they'd ever understood each other.

"I came back to make the end easier for you. For you and for Mom."

"I don't understand what you're saying, Luke."

His son pulled a small handgun from his belt. "When the time comes, you're going to have to be strong. Knowing Dara has gone ahead, maybe that will make what you'll have to do ... maybe it will be a little easier."

Luke placed the handgun on the ledge of the fire pit beside his father. "That's not for fighting off aliens, is it?"

His son shook his head. "If and when the time comes, I want you to have mercy. I don't want you to suffer."

"Suffer slow starvation or radiation burns or — "

"Didn't Mom say not to be morbid? Just don't put it off so long you can't use it, okay? No cowardice. Mom first, then you. When you do it, don't drag it out or say goodbye. Let it happen while she's asleep. Understand?"

This kid keeps forgetting I'm old, but I'm still much smarter than he ever was, Kurt thought. *And he's won the lottery while we're just the poor folks he's leaving behind.*

Kurt said nothing and managed a small smile of acknowledgment. "Don't worry, Luke. You can forge bravely into the future knowing you've got a clean slate and a clear conscience. No worries about your mom and me. We'll be fine. Thank you so much."

I hope you go to the safety of the mountain. And I hope they don't let you back in.

Kurt pocketed the weapon and stood. His low back, warmed by the fire, felt like it had a spring in it. Or maybe that was adrenaline doing its job, pumping him up with the fight or flight response. The trouble was, there was nowhere to run and no way to fight. If the aliens didn't kill him, the overly optimistic dolts with planet-destroying weapons surely would finish him off.

"We have hours until dawn," Luke said. "What do you want to do?"

As they headed into the house, Kurt clapped his son on the back. "I think we should follow Oscar Wilde's advice. We'll live life to the fullest while we still can. I propose we take a couple of candles, run down to the basement, and pop open the freezer. We need to eat as much of the ice cream we can before it melts. Thanks to you, I'm not worried about my weight or my blood pressure anymore."

"Will you drink a glass of wine with me?" Luke asked. "To toast Dara?"

"Sure," Kurt said. "A toast for Dara." *Nothing more suitable for the terrible loss of our daughter and your sister. An empty gesture I'll hate.*

"Thanks, Dad." Luke hurried ahead to fetch his father a wine glass.

"I'm so much stronger than you know," Kurt murmured, almost to himself. "I have such impressive fortitude, I'm not shooting you in the back of the head."

Luke stopped at the stairs to the front door and turned. "You say something?"

"Nothing! Coming! Coming!" Then Kurt muttered, "You smug prick."

Luke whirled on him. "What's up, Dad? If you've got something to say, say it!"

As his shame battled with his anger, Kurt stared at the ground. "It's not really about you, son. In light of current events, I've come to a realization. I have always thought of your mother and me as accomplished people. I guess I was kind of thinking the world revolved around us. Now it seems that if I had never been born, the world would look pretty much the same. That's the human condition, I guess."

Luke stepped forward to embrace his father. "What matters is what you did while you were here. Your life made a big difference to me. I'm here."

That didn't provide the depth of solace Luke thought it did, but Kurt didn't tell him how angry he was. He held back on revealing the depth and darkness of his envy. Instead, Kurt hugged his son and told him he loved him.

This, he thought, *is part of the human condition, too.*

V

Less time increases focus and clarity.

WHAT BINDS US

The prisoner's name was Andrew Fern, but everybody called him Red. Some called him the yard philosopher, but those weren't fellow inmates whom Red considered friends. He'd been an inmate at Kern Valley State Prison for twenty-seven years. In failing health, Red didn't think he'd make it to his next parole hearing. When the power went out, the dialysis machine's cycle abruptly stopped. Though his kidneys were the problem, Red felt like someone had punched him in the gut.

The machine died and I'm next, he thought.

Plunged into darkness in the windowless room, his heart began to pound. "Mr. Granger! The machine isn't working!"

"Nothing's working but me," the correctional officer replied. "Relax. The backup will kick in. Give it a minute."

"Shouldn't the power be back up right away, ASAP, and PDQ?"

That was true, but Granger sounded unconcerned. "Nurse Kelly will be back in a minute, Red."

But Amanda Kelly did not return. Neither did the prison doctor, Ian Munson.

Red appealed to the guard again, "Mr. Granger? What's going on?"

"No sirens, so it's not a break or a riot."

"Has anything like this happened before?" Red asked nervously.

The guard said nothing. Perhaps to save face, Granger waited another few minutes before trying his radio. "Central? This is Granger with one in the infirmary. Come back?"

His radio was as dead as the dialysis machine. His personal phone didn't work, either, not even its flashlight function.

Red was antsy. "Bad luck is what it is. I can feel it. Bad luck and worse coming. Story of my life."

"Stay put, Red. I'll find out what's going on."

"I still got a needle stuck in me. Where am I gonna go with my blood fillin' up with piss?"

Granger felt his way to the infirmary door and stuck his head out into the corridor. The shouts of the inmates reached him. He couldn't make out any words, but gauging by the angry tone, they weren't happy. The gen pop blocks were farthest from the infirmary, so he guessed the white-collar convicts in the Spoiled Brat Unit were upset the power outage had messed with their TV privileges.

Granger made his way down the hallway to the secure door and peered through the little window made of strengthened plexiglass and reinforced with wire. It had been a bright sunny day. Now it was almost seven p.m. With not even a sliver of ambient light, it may as well have been midnight in the belly of an enormous beast. Granger pounded on the door, but no one answered.

He'd been a guard for six years. Granger prided himself on not being easily rattled. At first, he'd taken the power outage as an oddity, nothing more. When the backup generator failed to pop on the emergency lights, that was cause for mild concern. The fact that no alarms sounded had been comforting. Then sober second thought crept in to sow doubt. *Lockdown alarms should go off. If this is a break, that would be a first. And here's me babysitting an old man, away from the action.*

Granger didn't love his job. However, when shit went down, he had the reputation of being the first to take the initiative, jump in, and solve problems. He'd always backed his crew, even the guards he didn't like. His philosophy was that every prison has gangs. As long as the guards were the toughest among them, the prison ran according to expectations.

Standing in the dark listening to distant shouting, he felt alone for the first time. Granger had never been out of communication before. Whatever was going on, things were not working as they should. *Red has a bad feeling. Me, too.*

As if in answer to the thought, the building shook hard. Thinking an earthquake had hit, Granger rushed back down the hallway. The rumbling stopped before he got back to the clinic door. He'd planned to stand in the doorframe. He was relieved the shaking and rocking had ceased, of course. However, the sudden stop left the guard bewildered.

A sound he'd never heard before came to him. It was neither an earthquake nor was it an explosion. The low rumble was interspersed with the shrieks of rended metal.

"Granger! Hey, Granger!" Red called into the darkness. "What the hell is going on?"

The guard muttered, "I do hate a mystery." He tried his radio again. No contact, not even static. He returned to the infirmary.

"Red? Sound off!"

"Still here, shittin' big ole bricks. What was that?"

"Like nothing I've ever heard. How about you?"

"Whatever it is, it ain't natural."

Already knowing the answer, Granger ventured, "So, not an earthquake?"

"Lived in California my whole life," Red replied. "If that was the big one, it was too short. If it was a little one, what was all that noise about? Sounded like ... metallic thunder. *Heh.* Metallic thunder. Was that a hair metal band from the '80s?"

Granger ignored his prisoner's question and walked deeper into the room. He accidentally kicked a chair. It rolled away into the pitch darkness.

"Stub your toe, Mr. Granger?"

"I'm fine. Actually, no. Not fine. Annoyed is what I am." Granger would not confess to worrying. Weakness could never be shared with an inmate, even one as feeble and well-behaved as Red Fern.

"C'mon now. You must know somethin'. What's the news?"

"There is none."

"That is news, just all bad and not particularly informative. So? What's the plan, chief?"

"We sit tight."

"Beautiful. Beautiful bad luck is what it is."

"What's the matter, Red? Afraid of the dark?"

"Yes, I am."

"Really?"

"Afraid so, I'm scared of the dark. Scared to the tits."

"Yeah? Why's that?"

"Because that's when they come for you."

"Nobody's coming for you, Red. I'm babysitting, so you know everything's going to stay kosher, cool, and five-by-five."

The prisoner's voice shook. "Somethin' already came for me, and you, too. Can't you feel it?"

"I don't know what you're talking about, but I don't even bother reading my horoscope, either."

"No? Why not, chief?"

"Because if I get a bad prediction, it might ruin my day or weaken my resolve to have a decent day. I don't let the stars dictate my mood. If anybody's going to ruin my day, it's going to be me or some convict who can't mind his p's and q's."

"You won't get no trouble from me, Mr. Granger."

"I know, Red. Maybe just sit there and take it easy, huh? We're waiting for instructions."

"What if the people you're waiting to hear from are waiting for instructions? What if everybody's like us and don't know jack shit? I've always suspected nobody but maybe a few geniuses really know what's goin' on."

"Red? *Sh!* You're giving me an ear beating and a pounding headache."

The prisoner tapped his toes on the tile floor. In the dark, every little noise seemed louder.

Uncomfortable with silence, Red could contain himself no longer. "I ain't sorry for talking. I'm all nervy over here. You haven't seen what I've seen, and now there's something out there tearing things up."

Granger had attended several mandatory training courses courtesy of California's penal system. Dealing with PTSD among inmates was a frequent topic. They were the sort of sessions that the more experienced and jaded guards openly mocked. However, Granger had once been in the Navy. There was something in the timbre of Red's voice that he recognized. The guard would never say he felt empathy for the old man, but the prisoner was his responsibility.

"You're mine, Red. I won't let anything happen to you. My feeling is there's an attempted escape going on. The way the building shook? Gotta be an underground explosion. Maybe some jackass tried to break out like El Chapo. If so, somebody's probably buried in a tunnel cave-in right now."

"But your radio doesn't work."

"Gotta be a jamming device. I visited Washington once. You couldn't use your cell phone in certain places. Same thing, I'm guessing."

"And the power outage?"

"The people trying to break somebody out must have cut the power. Every question has a logical answer. By now, help is on the way."

"You're so smart, what was that last sound? Like a million redwoods made of metal falling all at once."

Granger had no answer.

"Just guesses," Red said. "You don't know what's going on."

As genuinely afraid as his prisoner sounded, the anonymity of darkness served the correctional officer. In the pitch black, Red couldn't see the worried look on his keeper's face. It wasn't just the lack of communication from the control hub that bothered the guard. What of the other guards on his watch?

Kern Valley held almost 2,500 inmates in maximum security. With the power out and communications down, his fellow officers were in danger. It seemed Red's nervous energy had infected him.

It's true, I don't know what's going on. That's not acceptable. "Know what? We're going to get out of here."

"Got a bus to catch, Mr. Granger?"

"Can you yank out your line?"

To get out of the building, the pair had to pass through two doors. Before they could clear those hurdles, Red was forced to pull the line from the kidney dialysis machine. Since he had a port, that didn't turn into the ordeal the corrections officer expected. However, when the prisoner attempted to get into his wheelchair in the dark, he landed on the floor with a heavy thud.

"Red? You okay?"

"You forgot to lock the wheels."

Granger had never apologized to an inmate for anything, and he wasn't about to start. Instead, he felt his way through the dark room. He began to help the old man up from the floor, but Red stopped him. "Lock the wheels first, dumbass."

"You feeling feisty? I like it better when you call me Mr. Granger."

"That was before I found out how you people run your business. While we're flailing around in the dark, somebody's probably escaping. Tomorrow they'll be down at the Denny's enjoying Moons Over My Hammy."

Granger chuckled. "You like that stuff?"

"Never had it, but we talk about it. I'm too old to talk about women, but me and some of the older fellas discuss the places we've been and the food we loved. Mostly, us bein' us, we talk about where we'd like to go and the food we'd like to try. I spend a lot of my time thinking and talking about all the things I can't do. Nothin' changes. I did the same on the outside, too. That's one of the reasons I'm in here."

With some effort, the corrections officer helped Red back into the chair. The inmate's body was so warm and wet with sweat, it felt like the old man had a fever. Granger stepped back and wiped his hands on his pants.

Breathing heavily, Red asked, "What's next? High jump? Steeplechase?"

"You okay?"

"Do I sound okay? I wouldn't be so far gone except they spread out my dialysis appointments as long as they could. I should have been in here yesterday. Better yet, they should have let me out on a medical exemption. You ever get into trouble, hire your own lawyer. The free ones provided by the State will cost you long in the hind end. They're either too weak, too busy, or too not there for you at all. Story of my life."

Granger barely paid attention to his prisoner's complaints. What he was about to do would require patience, and he didn't have much left in the budget to hear a convict whine about how terrible the world had been to him.

The corrections officer approached the door Nurse Kelly had disappeared through. She'd left for a smoke break in the parking lot about twenty minutes before the lights went out. He found the door frame. The electronic lock was dead, of course, so his keycard was useless. There was a mechanical lock in the door, however. He carried several keys on the ring hooked to his belt. Granger just had to find the narrow slot of the key in the dark. The process was slow.

Red sat in his wheelchair, listening to the rattle of keys with increasing impatience. "Once, a long time ago, my father drove me home from someplace. Don't remember where. Anyway, I was little, but I have a clear memory of him standing next to our old blue van in the street. He locked the driver's door as he got out and slammed the door on his right thumb."

Granger, blind and fumbling to find the lock, answered with a disinterested grunt.

"When my father slammed that door on his thumb, he let out a string of curses. I never thought of my father as a poet, but when he got to cursing up a storm, the sky rained hot with bad words. He was *creative*. Man, it's amazing all the nearby churches didn't melt from the heat."

"Uh-huh."

"Anyway, that wasn't the fun part," Red said. "The fun part was that he had the keys in his jacket pocket by his right side! Get it? Right thumb stuck and he's howling like a werewolf in a movie, you know? Between all the cursin', that is."

"So? You reached into his pocket for him, used the keys, and freed the werewolf?"

"No," Red said flatly.

"You didn't want to be your dad's hero when you were a little kid?"

"My father was no hero. They say karma is a bitch, but that's the only evidence of justice I ever saw, inside a courtroom or out. I watched him howl for a long time. I watched him struggle, tryin' hard to reach those keys, all the while screaming and screaming at me."

"Were you born bad, Red?"

"Nobody's born bad, dumbass. You can be born stupid, dangerously impulsive, maybe ... but nobody's born bad. Bad isn't born. Bad is taught. It's *learned*."

"So, your dad was bad and taught you to be bad, huh? Boo-hoo. Plenty of people with bad dads don't end up in jail."

"It's worse than you're thinkin'. My father taught me to be scared. He's the one who locked me in a closet while he went off to work. Sometimes he left me something to eat or drink. Sometimes not. Sometimes not for a long time. You want someone to be really bad, teach them to be scared first. That man taught me how to be scared of the dark and to be terrified of tight spaces. Mostly, my father taught me to hate him."

The guard had heard many sob stories. Somehow, Red's nostalgia for revenge and sadism sounded different in the dark, more genuine and less performative. The old man sounded like a voice on the radio telling him a story. It was almost as if Red had become a voice in Granger's head.

"Not everybody's cut out to be a parent, I guess," the corrections officer observed.

"Parent? Lot of 'em are barely human beings."

"I know, I know," Granger sighed. "I meet a lot of people who are barely human in my line of work."

"You get to go home after your shift, maybe even eat at Denny's," Red replied. "I gotta live with them."

"If you ever get out, don't eat the Moons Over My Hammy. The sirloin steak is the best thing on the Denny's menu."

"I'm not telling you how to run your business," Red said, "but wouldn't one master key for the whole place make more sense?"

"More efficient, but less security," Granger said.

"Do you feel secure here in the dark with me? What if I was somebody else, say twenty years younger, a foot taller, and fifty pounds heavier?"

"And with a couple of kidneys that worked? Yeah, then I'd bother with handcuffs. I'd have to be meaner. You know our policy."

"'Be sweet to us, and we'll be sweet to you,'" Red quoted. "The warden gives that same speech to all the new fish. It's a lie. Heard that same shit on the outside, too. If I was a dumbass like you, I woulda believed people held to the Golden Rule. Maybe then I'd be the one trying to find a key to a lock in the dark. Maybe I'd be thumbin' and fumblin' around like a drunk comin' home at two in the morning, trying to get into the house without waking up the wife."

The correct key finally slid into the lock and turned the bolt. Granger got to his feet. "You sound out of breath from all that chirping. Ready to go, convict?"

"Praise Jesus, pass go, and do not go to jail. Be sweet to me, I'll be sweet to you."

The next room was part locker room and part lounge for the doctor and nurse. Granger had never once seen the nurse in there or even use the electric coffee pot. However, Dr. Munson used it as his office to make notes.

Granger held the door open. The chair's wheels scraped against the door frame as Red pushed through. The next room was as dark as the infirmary had been.

The corrections officer rushed in the direction of the exit door and banged his shin on a low table. He cursed as he rubbed his leg.

"Take it a little slower," Red suggested. "We've only got one wheelchair, and I'm not inclined to share."

"There's one more door to the parking lot."

"I don't like the dark, but I have a hard time with heat, too. Think Miss Kelly or Dr. Munson will let me sit in their car and enjoy some air conditioning?"

"Doubtful, but one step at a time, Red."

Granger found his way to the door and repeated the same arduous procedure as he had with the first door. As the minutes ticked by, he was thwarted with every attempt. *How do blind people do this?* he wondered.

With practice, he got better at finding the lock and sliding each key in as far as it would go. He began to suspect he didn't have the right key at all. Perhaps the lock had been changed, and his key ring was out of date. Or, more likely, the staff had been using key cards on the electronic lock for years without incident. It was possible Granger had never been issued a key to the outer door.

"How's it going, Boss?"

"About as well as it seems."

"I've been thinking, Mr. Granger. I don't much care for it in here, but maybe we don't want to rush out there. We don't know what we're getting into. That sound is haunting me like a nightmare after too much Halloween candy."

Granger stood suddenly and slammed the door with his open palm. Then he rammed it with his shoulder. The door did not move, but his shoulder hurt badly. "Damn it! I should be out there! I — "

The deadbolt turned with a scrape, and the door slowly opened. Amanda Kelly stood at the top of the steps. The nurse's scrubs were covered in dirt, and her red eyes told Granger she'd been crying.

"Miss Kelly?" Red asked softly. "What's up?"

She shook her head and stared into the eyes of the corrections officer. Granger sensed she barely registered his presence.

"What's going on, Amanda?"

"You won't believe it," she whispered. "You'll have to see it."

"Who did what to you?" Red persisted. "Mr. Granger will kick their asses, and I'll bring the popcorn."

The nurse shook her head again and beckoned for Granger to follow. Red was already wheeling through the door so the guard fell in behind him to push. They emerged on a ramp at the rear of the infirmary.

Amanda stood in the parking lot by her little red Toyota. She lit up a cigarette and gestured for Granger to go around the front of the infirmary.

"Why the mystery? What am I looking for?"

She uttered a bitter laugh. "You know when you ask someone for directions and they say, 'You can't miss it,' but obviously you can? You can't miss this."

Granger saw the big gray ship before he got to the front of the building. Lying on its side, the hulk had crushed the outer perimeter fence. The hull was snapped in two as if giant hands had broken a twig in half.

Granger recognized the design for what it was: an American naval ship. "Constellation-class," he muttered. "A frigate."

Red rolled up beside him and stopped abruptly. The prisoner let out a low whistle. "I've had some surprises in my time. The cops showing up at the worst time was one surprise. Finding out my best friend was a federal agent was a big surprise. This tops it all. That is one big boat! We are more than a hundred miles from the ocean. How the hell — "

"I can't see which one it is from here, but there should be 200 crew aboard."

"Should be?" Red marveled.

Where's the crew? Granger thought. *She's got a broken back and there's no crew!*

"We're way past what should be," Red continued. "We're in downtown Crazy Town! Don't know if anybody ever told you this, and I hate to be the one to say it, but that thing should be in the water."

"Shut it, Red."

Amanda walked up beside them, hugging herself. "I saw it happen. Nobody came out. The power went out, and a few minutes later, that happened."

Granger could not take his eyes off the ship.

"Miss Kelly? Please illuminate us."

"There were ships in the sky. Not like that. They were like nothing I'd ever seen. The top was smooth, but the bottom had all kinds of shapes, like buildings or maybe just, you know, protrusions like church spires. I don't know."

"Church spires? God's a far piece from this nonsense," Red said.

"Shut up!" Granger ordered. He nodded for the nurse to continue.

As Amanda Kelly took another long drag from her cigarette, her hands shook. "Lights in the sky zipping by. But this one aircraft, it was big with flashing red and green lights that went on and off, all over it. It was hard to look at directly. Too bright — "

"But the ship," Granger interrupted. "Tell me about the ship!"

"That's the thing. I was having a smoke when I looked up. It wasn't there and suddenly it was. Didn't make a sound, either. Just hovered with that ship beneath it. The thing in the sky lowered the navy ship to the ground so gently, I thought it would stand straight, marooned on land, you know? Then the thing began to slide, and it made an awful racket when it fell over."

"And nobody's come out?"

"Dr. Munson went to see."

"And?"

"He wasn't gone long. When he came back, all he told me there was mush and blood everywhere. Our phones don't work. Neither do our cars. Then Ian left."

"The doctor *left*? Well, screw me, I guess," Red said.

"He said I should go, too," Amanda said. "I was just taking a few minutes to have a couple of cigarettes, and, you know, rethink everything I thought I knew. I said ships, but let's face facts. Those were UFOs I saw."

"And we're under attack," Granger concluded. "That's an act of war and man, oh, man, are we ever outgunned. Gotta be. We've got nothing that could lift a whole ship in the air like that."

"Well, shit," Red said. "Can you beat that? The answer, lady and gentleman, is no."

"What was the question?" Nurse Kelly asked.

"I know when quitting time is and this is it! From what you describe, I'm betting the crew of the USS Broken Egg there died from the sudden start or the sudden stop. The little green men neglected to tell those sailors to fasten their seatbelts. No airbags on a boat like that."

The corrections officer tore his gaze from the wreckage and turned his fury on his prisoner. "Don't enjoy this, Red! Don't you dare enjoy this!"

"I'm not, Mr. Granger. It's just that I figure I'm dead by tomorrow or so anyway. God has granted me a wish."

If he hadn't been so old and frail and sitting in a wheelchair, Granger would have hit him. He wanted to. It was really only Amanda Kelly's presence that held him back. "This is your father's thumb stuck in the van door all over again, isn't it? If you laugh, I will toss you out of that chair and stomp you, I swear to God!"

"Aim for my kidneys," Red said evenly. "They really only serve a decorative purpose now, anyways."

Granger grabbed the arm of the wheelchair, intent on flipping Red to the ground. Amanda stepped forward and stopped him.

"I ain't laughing," Red protested. "I didn't laugh at my father's pain, either! You said I laughed. I never said I laughed. I have never laughed at another person's pain. I've felt too much of it myself to take any joy in it. If I made the world, there'd be no pain."

Granger knelt beside the old man, his voice low and threatening. "You said God granted you a wish." He pointed to the wreckage before them. "And?"

Red gave a slow nod. "When my father got his thumb smashed in the door and couldn't get out, I was not laughing at him. I was seeing something I thought I'd never see. My tormentor was helpless."

"And?"

"You never treated me very bad or very good, but sure as shit you never saw me as a human being. Seeing you like this against forces that can pick up a warship and drop it where they want? You're finally like me."

"Oh? I don't think so."

"Sure you are. Maybe you don't see it yet, but you're helpless. You're as vulnerable as me. I was kinda hopin' you'd finally understand how I feel all the time. You want to do something, Mr. Granger. I get that, but what is there to do? May as well argue with the rain. You know the old joke about the 500-pound gorilla? What do you give him? Whatever he wants. Now think aliens instead of gorilla and you'll pick up what I'm layin' down."

Granger's fury drained away along with his energy. He stood and returned to gaze at the broken hulk of the ship. He'd been a seaman on a frigate like that once briefly before he served aboard the *Carl Vinson*, an aircraft carrier.

"People who don't know helplessness act like assholes," Red continued. "Of course, if you make people helpless for too long, they get to acting like assholes, too." The prisoner shot his nurse a grin. "People are people and few escape that curse. That's how I ended up here actually."

At that moment, five correctional officers emerged from Building G. As soon as they spotted the trio standing in front of the infirmary, one split off from the group and jogged over. "Hey, Granger! Can you believe this shit?"

Greg Crawley was one of the youngest guards on staff. He wasn't merely excited. The man looked weirdly cheerful as he pointed to the wrecked ship. "I saw it happen. I was walking the perimeter when this huge UFO appears in the sky right over there!"

"Nurse Kelly told me," Granger replied. "What's happening on the inside?"

"Power's out."

"That, I know. Are they locked down?"

"I guess the first few minutes after the lights went out, it got a little hairy. The boys got geared up for a riot, but when I told everybody what I saw, things quieted down. Like, really quiet. They're all talking to each other, exchanging conspiracy theories, I think."

Granger waved toward the guards who were leaving. "What's the deal with them?"

"We asked the warden for leave to go check on our families. Radio, TV, and internet are all dead. We're supposed to find out what's going on and report back."

"How are you supposed to do that?" Amanda asked.

Crawley shrugged. "Ask around, I guess. Somebody has to know something. If somebody has a working radio, we're supposed to call the FBI or the governor's office or — "

"Ghostbusters?" Red chuckled. "A big ass Navy ship drops from the sky by an even bigger ass UFO! You think the governor knows what to do about that?"

Crawley ignored the prisoner and looked to Granger. "You don't live far. You wanna go ask the warden for leave and — "

"No. I don't think I need to ask permission. That's all over. Everything we thought we knew is over. Go home, Greg. If I were you, I don't think I'd put a high priority on rushing back here."

Crawley looked mystified, but bobbed his head and followed the other guards toward the front gate.

"That young fella is kinda slow on the uptake and significance, isn't he?" Red observed.

Overhead, the first star appeared in the darkening sky. Granger stared at it. "Since I was a little kid I wanted to be part of something larger. I found that feeling of belonging in the Navy. Had it here, too. Now that I know there is alien life and ... I feel ... I don't know what I feel."

"Smaller," Red said. "You feel smaller. I know that feeling well. It comes to the party with helplessness. Despair is on its way, too, fashionably late, but a-comin'."

Amanda stood beside Granger. "What should we do?"

"Nothing to do. All at once, everything has changed. Just like that, everything, everything."

"Feels like we've been hit by a car," Amanda added, "except it's the whole world."

Red cleared his throat. "Wanna go to Denny's?"

Granger turned to Amanda and Red. "Why not? Looks to me like we're all condemned prisoners now."

Red smiled. "And condemned prisoners get a fancy last meal."

"I don't know how fancy it will be, or how bad it will screw up your blood — "

"Don't care!" Red said.

"What if the power's out at the restaurant, too, though?" Amanda asked.

"My house is closer. Sirloin steaks in the fridge. It's not Denny's, but the propane grill should work fine."

"Then what?" Amanda asked.

"Enjoy the meal first in the open air and love the fact you're still breathin'," Red suggested. "Take it from me, stay stuck in the past and you get depressed. Worry all the time about the future, you get anxiety. I got pretty uptight before. I didn't like being stuck in the dark. Seein' that ship, I got some perspective back."

The corrections officer frowned. "The crew are dead and you're not, so you're happy?" It was more of an accusation than a question.

"Why not? I'm not happy they're dead, mind you. I am pleased to live long enough to see a big change comin'. We die and we're forgotten and that's everybody! Nobody gives a shit about your regrets. Your good deeds get forgotten, too. I've been judged as if people are all bad or all good. To see this besides four gray walls before I go, that's really somethin'!"

Amanda looked at Red doubtfully. "Yeah? What's so great about it?"

"The people who think they're so high and mighty will be brought low," Red replied. "The people who thought they were so much better than me will do things they never thought they would. Best of all, the people in power will lose it. They made folks like me their enemy. Now they've got someone new to hate."

"He's not wrong," Granger said. "I already hate the aliens more than Red."

Red nodded. "He gets it. Tell me, Mr. Granger, what's your first name?"

"Ted."

"I am filled with awe at this odd turn of events!" Red said. "Miss Kelly, Ted, and Red went home for dinner at the end of the world. Sweet!"

Amanda gave the corrections officer a hard look. "You sure you're okay with this? Letting a prisoner escape? To your home, no less?"

He nodded. "Dying men get the last meal they want, and I want a steak."

VI

We crave change.
We fear change.
We don't change.

WHAT WE NEED

As daylight leaked around my blackout curtains, I broke the fuzzy boundary of sleep and began the arduous return to consciousness. I suddenly became acutely aware of my spine. It wasn't pain, but in my mind's eye, I could see and feel every bone, nerve, blood vessel, and intervertebral disc. Every articulation felt uneasy, as if something might crumble or break and I'd fall to the floor, a boneless heap of meat in the clothes I'd slept in.

Oh, I thought. *I'm still a little high.*

A chronic insomniac, I'd long used a THC and CBD spray to help me sleep. After the events of the night before, I'd used much more of the spray than usual. The little canister had been light as I held the peppermint elixir under my tongue.

An old, bald guy named Mort worked at the dispensary in Salem. Standing behind the sales counter, he always wore a Sponge Bob pajama top. I hoped he did so ironically. Mort had advised me that my mix was strong and to use just a few pumps of the spray under my tongue. "Someday," he said, "I'm gonna try the whole canister at once to see what happens."

"Whoa! Pull back on the throttle there, doctor! I'm just trying to get some decent sleep! I'm not trying to rocket to space."

But I'd changed my mind after the events of the night before. Staying up listening to my dad's old ham radio, I'd become a bundle of nerves, hot and electric. Far-flung contacts from around the world told me aliens had arrived on Earth, and the space invaders were not friendly.

I crawled into my bed at dawn and slept until noon. Safe and cozy in my bed with my afghan pulled up under my nose, all that seemed like a very improbable nightmare. Twisting the old ham radio's dial, I'd searched for threads of news from a blanket of static. At first, the idea of an interplanetary war sounded kind of amusing, maybe even a solution to mankind's problems.

Man isn't all that kind. A common enemy might be just the thing to finally unite us.

However, as the night wore on, good sense took over and my dread grew. Between sips of beer, I told myself it had to be some spectacular hoax. However, cannabis is not acid. The fear in the voices reporting in felt too real. This wasn't a movie. The attack was real.

Last night I spoke to a frantic air traffic controller at JFK. That happened.

I pulled the afghan over my head and snuggled into my cocoon even deeper. The bed was so comfortable, it felt like I was nestling into a cloud of warm goodness. However, dimly aware that I'd been dreaming about peeing, I had to get to the toilet.

Go on! I told myself. *Get your lazy ass to challenge gravity.*

Moving gingerly, I struggled to get out of bed. Bleary, stiff, and barefoot, I forced myself to pad across cold floors to get to the bathroom. I was finishing up at the toilet when someone began pounding on my back door. I parted the Venetian blinds with my free hand and peered out the window. "What?"

"Uncle Kent!"

My sister's kid, Jordan "Cyclops" Murray was at my back door. She looked up at me, her one good eye was a piercing ice-blue. "What's the latest? Have you heard anything more?"

I zipped up and cranked the bathroom window open. "What have *you* heard?"

"Power's still out all over town."

"All over everywhere," I said. "Everything's all over. We should eat something before the end of the world is official. The key is under the flower pot. I'll be down in a minute."

"Which flower pot? There are no flowers, just pots."

"The terracotta one that was supposed to grow something-or-other and didn't."

I cranked the window shut and turned to the sink. A rueful glance in the mirror told me I was looking older than I should. My reflection was both disappointing and disappointed. My eyelids were red and itchy, and I'd run out of eye drops.

J'accuse, numbnuts! You're suddenly running out of time. Meant for great things, never got around to it. Put that on the tombstone. That's the only mark you'll make.

"You were once bound for great things," I scolded my reflection. "Everybody said you were going to be a great screenwriter. And now it's the end of the friggin' world. *Jeez!* One part bad luck, two parts laziness! And now it's all self-loathing. Way to go, champ!"

Movies had been my passion. I studied film at Chapman University. Upon graduation, I was almost a hot property. My script about a romance between two poor teens in rural Oregon got passed around from producer to producer, studio to studio. I went from hot to cold after a series of near misses.

Agatha, my agent, was a hitter in the movie business and burbled with praise over the script I sent her. At least, she was enthusiastic at first.

"This is good," she'd told me as she flipped through my latest draft. "You have a good ear for dialogue, really got those hick voices down."

"Heard those voices all my life."

"Just one more rewrite," she'd told me.

I groaned at that suggestion, dramatically and unprofessionally.

"Well, not so much a rewrite as a different approach."

I groaned louder.

Agatha winced and peered over her glasses at me with a new

look, severe and displeased. "This is the way it is, Kent. Try this on for size. Make the lovers a couple of sophisticates in their mid-twenties. One of them should be a billionaire's heir or heiress, doesn't matter which. Also, set it in Tuscany. Actors and directors love to work in Tuscany."

"Are you kidding me?"

"I know you can do it. Just a couple more notes. Trust me, your script is a bit too gritty. People are sick of gritty. They want sunshine and fantasy right now, or at least they will two to five years from now if the project gets greenlit and all the variables come together."

"Agatha, what I wrote was packed with truth — "

"Give them a lie they can love, instead. Lies, I can sell. Get some success under your belt, pay your dues, and maybe we can revisit the sad hicks in Oregon. You have the skill. Just give me something I can sell instead of hunting for Oscar bait right out of school. Trust me, people hate prodigies. They love workhorses."

"I gave you a police procedural about people disappearing in rural Oregon. You want overprivileged brats falling in love in Tuscany? I've never been to Tuscany!"

"Google it."

I let out another long sigh. I should have known better, but I didn't think of myself as the hack writer they wanted. I thought of myself as the *artiste* they needed.

"Listen, I need a writer. The market wants a fairy tale. End it on page 129 with a glorious wedding and happily-ever-after. What you wrote works on the page, but the father's suicide is a heavy ending. The question you have to ask yourself is, do you want to follow your passion or do you want to follow me? Follow my lead, you'll make movies, and not incidentally, *money*."

"I was just trying to write something true," I told her.

My agent laughed. "You're already getting a little old to be a kid, Kent! People don't want the truth. They only say they do. This is the way it is."

This is the way it is. Six words that mean give up and do as you're told. Don't try for more, settle for less. Give up trying to make things better.

Depressed and exhausted from the never-ending dance, I moved back home to Knock Station, Oregon, the scene of my parents' original sin. Original Sin was Dad's nickname for me. He also mentioned offhandedly that I was conceived in front of the fireplace.

Josh, my roommate and fellow film school graduate, asked if I was okay with moving back in with my father. "A big part of your script is about achieving escape velocity from your hometown. Now you're moving back there?"

"This is the way it is," I said.

"Bad move, man!" Josh replied. "Live in your car and get a job at Red Lobster with me. The debt collectors can't find you if you live in your car."

Of course, I wasn't fine with moving back into my childhood bedroom and living with my father. We weren't on the same page politically. However, I rationalized that I could work on rewrites from anywhere. Living thirty-five miles from Hollywood put me no closer to working in the movie business than living 913 miles away. Rent in Los Angeles piled on top of my crushing student loan debt made the decision to run home easier.

With the disastrous news from the airwaves, at least I wouldn't have to worry about paying back those student loans.

Thanks, killer aliens!

I descended the stairs to find Cyclops pouring herself a bowl of Cheerios.

"Sorry, I'm out of that fake milk you like," I told her.

"It's okay. I like 'em dry."

"You tell your parents to stock up on groceries and whatnot?"

"First thing, but they don't believe me."

The kid was kind enough to say her parents didn't believe her. The truth was my sister Catherine wouldn't believe anything coming out of my mouth. She married a plumber who made big bank so they were comfortable. I'm in the failed screenwriter business, so why would she listen to me?

"The car doesn't work," Cyclops added, "so Mom said they can't go get groceries anyway."

I took a deep breath and held my tongue. At fourteen, Cyclops was a good kid with more sense than most adults I knew. Also, she loved my film script and passing that test proved she was among the best people in the world. However, her mother and I rarely saw eye-to-eye.

It frustrated me that Catherine and her husband Brian wouldn't walk three short blocks to the grocery store. Knock Station was not so much a small town, more of a wide spot in the road somebody decided to name. The Knock didn't even appear on some maps.

"A truck stop that puts on airs," my father used to say of the town. "Hang a left at Salem, head out on the 22 and don't blink. If you get as far as Lincoln City, keep driving your dumb ass straight into the ocean 'cuz you missed us."

In the Knock, nobody walked unless they had to. I would file our situation at that moment under "Had to." The trouble was that the news of an alien invasion was coming from me, not over the federal emergency alert system.

I understood my sister's disinclination to abide by my judgment. Folks around ol' Knock said I took after my dad. That was not widely considered a good thing. Some of the locals surely thought my father was crazy, but no one would have dared to say so to his face. Folks up our way are polite to those who stockpile guns. The worst they'd say to Chuck Schreiber was that he was anti-social.

Dad didn't attend church. When pressed by a well-meaning and oblivious neighbor, he replied, "Me and God, we disagreed to agree on the fine points. The big guy and me, we came to an understanding. We stay out of each other's way and keep our noses to our own business. I like it when people mind their own business."

Dad never darkened the door of the fire hall for the bean suppers, either. "Raising funds for the volunteer fire department is a fine thing for those who worry about their crap going up in flames," he said. "If our house goes up one day, I'll just throw my go-bag over one shoulder and you over the other and run for the woods."

My father was paranoid, but he hadn't expected aliens to come to colonize us. He called America's obsession with space, "Nothin' more than nerd shit. Don't believe the government's lies. The space program isn't about going to Mars. It's really about developing better killer robots, drones, and missiles. It's spy satellites that'll fry free-thinkers like me from high orbit." However, as long as I knew my father, he'd been sure something terrible was coming to get him ... and perhaps incidentally, everyone else, too.

Chuck Schreiber obsessed over many common dangers. Earth-quakes, forest fires, and mudslides usually topped his list of daily threats. He somehow convinced himself all those threats were immi-nent and likely, no matter how sunny the sky might be. Whatever disaster might befall us, he was betting heaviest on civil war.

"People laugh," he said, "but we already had one, and there's no bag limit on the number of revolutions any country is allotted."

He bet wrong, but he did have a touch of prescience beneath the conspiracy theories and anti-government rants. If he'd been sitting next to his little ham radio with me through the night, he would have cracked open a beer, clapped me on the back, and crowed, "Finally! Told you so!"

After all the dire messages transmitted through the night, Dad would have been excited to finally get the apocalypse underway. He would have grabbed a rifle and faced the alien threat with me. However, whatever plans the little green men had for us, I'd have to face the danger without my father. Sadly, the only threat Dad didn't take seriously was the pandemic. He convinced himself it was another government lie. That's how his lungs turned to quick-setting cement.

I didn't get to see my father in the ICU in Salem. When I asked, his nurse said his last words were, "Tell my kids I love them."

I pressed, "Yeah, yeah, what did he really say?"

She let out a long sigh and confessed, "Chuck's exact words were a whisper. 'Put a round in my head and be done with it.'"

The nurse then added, "The body's systems work to sustain life as long as possible. When certain things go awry, the cascade of organ failures hits quickly."

"Failure follows the men in my family," I told her. "Follows us like stink."

I'm embarrassed to admit that my father's death made me worry more about my own. Being a prepper and a conspiracy theorist was Dad's entire personality. That image defined him. I feared I'd be defined as the kid who left the Knock for Hollywood and returned a failure.

In a small town, once a mold is set, it's hard to break. If people knew you when you were in diapers, they always figure they're ahead of you, smarter, and better. I imagined people in town talking amongst themselves. "There goes Chuck Schreiber's kid. Went to Hollywood to make movies and now he's back. Guess he wasn't as smart as he thought he was."

Some nights I'd lie awake worrying about the future. Seemed like a lot of wasted time since an invasive species from the stars arrived. Based on my radio conversations through the long night, power grids, communications, and faith that we'd live to see another day all proved surprisingly vulnerable.

An alien invasion surely does put my little life in perspective. I hate perspective.

A political dissident in Hong Kong named Feng had shielded her radio from EMPs. She had expected communications arrays would be wiped out by the Chinese government prior to invasion from the mainland. That invasion did not come to pass. Instead, she was able to report an alien attack.

Feng told me she saw one enormous alien ship floating ominously overhead. Hong Kong's streets were full of rioters and celebrants, possibly in equal measure. What each side had in common was an enthusiasm for looting supplies from stores up and down her street.

Dad left me the house, the guns, ammunition, a stack of magazines about prepping, some seeds, and a Faraday cage for his ham radio. The magazines went mostly unread, and I never got around to starting the garden. Dad was most enthusiastic about cleaning the guns, target shooting, and trading conspiracy theories with other preppers from around the globe.

I wished Dad were with me. I couldn't bring myself to enjoy chaos, but my father loved disruption. Watching the news, Dad would sit in his recliner and mutter, "Everything's messed up. What this world needs is some shakin' up! The system is so weak, anything that takes down civilization is an opportunistic infection. I say somebody should Etch A Sketch this bitch and see what happens next! Some things you gotta shake up and break up before you can fix the problem."

An alien invasion is an earthquake to human consciousness. We surely needed a course correction, but not this.

I wished I'd listened to Agatha and stayed in L.A. I wished I'd written the hack say-nothing script she wanted. The colonizers had arrived on Earth, and all things considered, I'd rather die rich lounging in the Hollywood Hills beside a piano-shaped pool in a house that Bono used to own.

I looked around my shitty little house. Dad left it all to me because he knew my sister, Catherine the Great, didn't need any help. She got my late mother's jewels and a fancy dish set. The guns and the house were mine. At Dad's funeral, Catherine put a hand on my shoulder and whispered, "Don't worry about the will. I won't fight it."

"It didn't occur to me that you would. Dad told us both what he wanted before they put him on the ventilator."

Her expression was a coldly calculated mix of sympathy and condescension. "Saul's making good money, and it's not like I need that dusty old house. The taxes alone will probably sink you. I just wanted you to know I'm still your big sister. I understand your financial situation. You need the place more than I do, is all." Catherine rubbed my shoulder as if she were massaging salt into a wound.

When I left for Los Angeles, Catherine was jealous that I was the one escaping Knock Station. When I came back wearing the heavy shroud of failure, she was warm, welcoming, and happy for all the wrong reasons. I didn't realize that we were competing or how mean she could be. Not until she cast herself in the role of the long-suffering saint.

I used to want it all. Like that TikTok meme about all of the problems in the United States: "This is America." The pretty woman with the heavy New York accent I couldn't identify stared down the barrel of the camera and declared, "We're told we should want it all. Instead, we need to focus on being enough, not for others but for ourselves. Others don't care about you. I don't care about you. Nobody cares about you. Care for yourself. Be enough just for you. This is America."

She got a lot of hate in the comments for that message, but she went viral. The trolls came out to shout her down, but the flame war only made her more popular.

I wondered if that taste of success made that New Yorker feel like she was finally enough. She'd told the world that the American dream was a fraud in a rant that lasted less than a minute. In every TikTok video she'd made since, I had the impression she was still chasing virality, betraying her message, soliciting free samples from a soap company, and trying to get sponsored.

Jordan had been watching me as she ate her cereal. When she spoke, my trance shattered. "Uncle Kent? The power's out since last night, but not many people know what's going on yet."

"Yeah? So? What's the plan, Cyclops?"

She finished her Cheerios and put the bowl in the sink. "Cereal *is* better with almond milk. I say we go shopping while the shopping's good."

I perked up. "Retail therapy? Actually, that's a good idea! It's like we got an insider's stock tip."

"Pulled my old wagon out of the back of the garage," she said. "Let's load up on things we shouldn't eat."

"That and non-perishables," I said. "Your grandfather would insist we get a lot of spam."

My niece wrinkled her nose. "Nachos. No spam."

We enjoyed the advantage of being ahead of the curve for all of four minutes. The first spaceship flew over Northern Oregon as I was locking the front door. Jordan and I stood in the front yard, wordless and a little breathless, too. I'd listened intently to Feng's description of the ship over Hong Kong. Nothing could have prepared me for seeing the real thing.

The craft did not zip over us in a flash. In fact, the vehicle's movement was surprisingly slow. It didn't fly directly overhead. It was far away, but it still seemed huge. Jaws slack and gawking, we stood there like statues. The top of the ship was smooth and silver. An array of oddly shaped projections hung from the bottom of the craft.

"I never thought I'd see a UFO in the daytime or for so long," Jordan marveled. "And if I did see anything, I assumed it would zip across the sky like in that old movie you made me watch."

"Made you? Oh, yeah. You mean *Close Encounters of the Third Kind*." Jordan had fallen asleep on the couch halfway through the film.

"I've got a bad feeling about this," Jordan said.

"Me, too," I admitted. "Somehow, I guarantee these aliens aren't like the ones in the movie. There's something predatory about that thing, like whoever's aboard doesn't appreciate music nearly as much as the Greys in the movie."

"I didn't expect it to be so big," she said. "You said the woman from Hong Kong told you hers was big, but ... wow."

At that, I took a page from my father's book and ran back into the house. A few minutes later, I reemerged with a pistol tucked under my shirt in the small of my back. I carried Dad's favorite rifle, an M4A1.

Jordan didn't have to ask why I felt the need to carry. "It's going to get crazy from here on out, isn't it?" Hers was a statement, not a question.

I gave my niece a nod. It wouldn't do to tell her comforting lies. She was too smart for that, smarter than me.

"There was looting in Hong Kong," I said. "Things were always crazy, but I expect the stakes to climb up a few notches. If things get really crazy, I want you to run on home out of harm's way, yeah?"

The kid was the only family I had left whom I liked. I wanted to continue to be her cool uncle, so I didn't send Jordan home right away. I should have.

As we walked to the store, we passed people standing in their front yards. Some little kids shouted excitedly, running in circles. Most adults stood in silent shock. They stared up at the sky, craning their necks and pointing as if to reassure themselves they weren't the only ones seeing the UFO.

Jordan pulled her little red wagon. It was dirty and one of the tires squeaked. I'd pulled her around in it, back when she was a toddler and I wasn't day drinking.

Julie Wertley tore her gaze away from the alien ship and spotted me. "Hey, Kent! Do you suppose that thing is something new our side cooked up?"

Julie and I had been hot and heavy in high school for a couple of weeks. I always thought I owed her extra courtesy so, instead of hurrying on, I slowed enough to shake my head.

"Do you think it's from Russia or China or North Korea?" Julie asked.

I shook my head. "That thing is too big and too quiet to be from this planet."

Her latest boyfriend, Kyle Rickles, stood behind her. He would have been working at the gas station, but with no electricity to run the pumps, I guessed he'd come over to hang out with Julie.

Kyle called to me over Julie's hedge. "Hey! Schreiber! Aliens come to visit and the first thing you think is to grab your gun? You think you can defend Earth against aliens packing ray guns and shit?"

"Take it easy, Kyle," Julie warned.

Undeterred, Kyle announced to the neighbors, "Kent Schreiber, ladies and gentlemen! Hero and protector of us all! I think you've seen too many movies there, buddy!"

This was not the first time Kyle had chirped at me. He was a big guy, thick through the shoulders and arms in a way that suggested, despite the fat, he could be dangerous if he put his mind to it. He'd made it clear on numerous occasions that he didn't think much of my lifestyle. He was a working man, and I was worthless. I'd always smiled and given the man a wide berth. However, today was different. I strongly suspected it was the end of the world. At the end of the world, it doesn't do to leave something unsaid that needs to be said. Besides, I was carrying an M4A1, and that was A1 with me.

Instead of my usual tolerant smile and walking on, I came to a dead stop. I fixed him with my eyes. "Kyle, this is not a gun. A gun is a cannon. This is a lethal weapon. I understand if you do not respect me. I suspect you've got some motivated reasoning going on considering Julie and I used to date."

Julie's hands were fists. "Kent!"

"No offense or disrespect intended, Julie. It's just that your gentleman caller seems to have more of a hard-on for me than for you. That is somewhat inexplicable to me given what I know of you. You gave me a couple of the best weeks of my life. I thank you. And Kyle? You, I do not thank. "

Julie's face flushed beet red, but her hands weren't fists anymore. I like to think I gave her a couple of good weeks, too. Kyle just stood there, looking from me to the rifle in my hands.

"This isn't for defending Earth," I told him. "What kind of fantasy do you have about me thinking I would defend you from anything? This weapon isn't for aliens that get in my way, Kyle. *Not* for aliens, *get it?*"

He stepped behind Julie and slipped his arms around her.

My niece giggled. She looked to Julie. "You should dump him. Your guy got called out, and the first thing he did was use you as a human shield!"

Julie frowned and pushed Kyle away.

I grinned. "Feel that tension in the air? You could hear a pin drop!"

My niece squeezed my arm and urged me to walk on. "That wasn't a pin, Uncle Kent. Those were Kyle's balls hitting the ground."

I let out a guffaw. Kyle smoldered and burned but said nothing. Best of all, Julie burst out laughing.

Harv Whitley called from behind his fence across the street. "Hey! There's a huge spaceship crossing the sky! Anybody watching that?"

"Sorry to distract from the big show, Harv!" I called back.

"Show's over!" Kyle shouted.

By his eyes, I knew he wanted to beat my ass. I had the rifle, so his other option was to casually sashay back into Julie's house and pass off our confrontation as nothing. With an otherworldly mystery on display before our eyes, he couldn't very well do that, either. Satisfied Kyle's ego was sufficiently dented, I gave Jordan the nod and we walked on.

I hadn't felt so good in a long time. The way Julie looked at me made me feel warm. Riling up Kyle was a bonus that made me feel taller.

One of the things my father loved about living in Oregon was that it was an open-carry state. Now I understood why Dad never left the house without a pistol. When superiority can't be had, toting a lethal machine made by Colt served as a reasonable facsimile.

I asked him once why he bothered. He told me, "You never know when you're going to run into a varmint." Watching Kyle scurry to hide behind Julie's skirts, I understood my father a little better.

As we walked, my two eyes and my niece's one tracked the massive ship. "I'm assuming it didn't fly so slow on its way here," she said.

"Prolly not."

"Where do you suppose it came from?"

"Mars is overrated and everywhere else seems too far away, so it's hard to say. Nice to see somebody figured out space travel. If not for the massive power outage coinciding with their arrival, I'd like to think they're here to save us."

"From what?"

"Ourselves."

Jordan gave me a questioning look.

"There's an old adage," I said. "Something about how the kind of dumbass brains that create problems aren't up to fixing them. All we know is they figured out space travel. Funny how figuring out how to get from here to there changes everything. Airline travel shrank the world. That's amazing technology. The first flight and landing on the moon were only sixty-some years apart."

"Flying shrank the world?" Jordan asked.

"Well, yeah. Then the internet divided it."

"When the internet comes back, maybe we'll be able to put it back together again."

"That may be why the aliens took the internet away from us. It certainly wasn't to make friends. Take the internet away from anybody and they get real mad. Hard to imagine we ever got along without it."

All along the way, the townspeople had come out of their houses to stare up in awe. The craft moved so slowly, sometimes it looked like the alien ship had come to a complete stop.

"Where are our jets?" Jordan asked. "In the movies, they always send fighter jets to intercept the bogie."

I guessed our defenses had been crippled by the EMP. "Maybe the answer is in your question," I offered. "They're called fighter jets because they fight. What if the government doesn't want to come off as hostile to the aliens? Presumably, they don't know anything about the intruders. Maybe our side is waiting to see if they're just interstellar neighbors popping over for a cup of brown sugar. Cutting off our power could be an accident. Their engines could have interfered with us, and all they really want is to make chocolate chip cookies."

My father would have laughed at such a naive suggestion. "Not overreacting to a potential threat before we know our enemy? *Ha!*"

The dead dad of my imagination had a point. Showing restraint instead of a show of force would be a first.

When we arrived at the Knock's little grocery store, a few of our fellow townsfolk had the same idea as I did. Charlene Pino and her five boys had three small buggies full of canned goods and cereal. My third-grade teacher, Edna Greensby, trailed along behind the Pino family complaining that they should leave something for somebody else.

Edna had been an awful teacher, but that was only because she was an awful person. Long retired, she continued to inflict herself on Knock Station. We tended to grin and bear her abuse. That's the trouble with small towns. Everybody's a little too polite and tolerant.

The way Dad put it, "We're so nice and polite for fear the people we offend will outlive us. That's why I don't want a funeral. Soon as I lay down, all these cowards that talked shit about me behind my back for years will finally have the last word."

At my sister's insistence, we had held a funeral for my father anyway. All of Knock Station turned out for his send-off. Judging from the hushed conversations as I passed their little cliques, Dad wasn't wrong.

I bent to whisper in my niece's ear. "I think today is the day I take another page from your grandfather's book. This isn't a day to be too polite."

Jordan frowned so hard, the skin around her eye patch wrinkled. "The Dali Lama says to be kind when possible and it's always possible."

"The Dalai Lama has an entourage of monks who will feed him if things go sour. Have you got a platoon of monks looking after you?"

She shook her head ruefully.

"Then take what you want, preferably not too many perishables."

"Almond milk and nachos, though?"

"Yeah, you can have the almond milk and nachos."

Jordan slipped down the farthest aisle with her wagon, and I grabbed a basket. The Pino boys had only taken food they liked. I took their leavings.

The shop's owner, Burt Caldwell, stood behind the front counter looking glum. He was the sort of gangly old guy who moved slowly, as if all his joints ached. I only saw him stand straight if there wasn't anything nearby on which he could lean. Watching Edna Greensby harass the Pino family, he bent so far over the counter he looked like he was in the position to get a prostate exam. "Cash only today! Cash only!" he warned. "'Lectric's out so the cash machine don't work right."

"I don't imagine it works at all," Charlene Pino called back breezily. "The only ATM in town isn't working, either!"

"How do you propose to pay then?"

"Write it down. You'll have my IOU. You know I'm good for it!"

Edna Greensby cackled the way only witchy old smokers can.

"*IOU?* Give me a break! Kick 'em out of the store, Burt! These people are good for nothing."

I stepped in behind the youngest Pino boy to block Edna and let the family go about their business. "These people are just taking care of themselves, just like everybody else."

She pointed at the Pino kids. "They're trash. All this talk of aliens, but we should be calling Immigration on them."

"They're *people*," I replied. "Don't you wish *you* were human? You're one of *them*, aren't you?"

"W-what?" Edna cupped her hand to her ear. "You're not making any sense!"

"You're an alien. You came to Earth a thousand years ago to spy on us. This explains a lot. I'm sure you're a fine alien, but you're a shitty human."

She sputtered.

"That wrinkly old mask is slipping, Mrs. Greensby," I continued. "Return to the mother ship before I call the FBI and Immigration on *you!*"

The old woman stalked away to complain to Burt. He straightened enough to lean on the dead cash register. Wearing his most hangdog look, he shook his head in a way that conveyed commiseration, but he would do nothing for her.

I was 2 and 0 for telling off assholes in elegant ways, so I did not dally. Up and down the narrow aisles, I searched for essentials. Dad kept a big box of batteries in the basement, but I wasn't sure they still had much charge.

He kept a bunch of tins of food, too. However, since his death, I hadn't bothered to check the expiration dates and had failed to rotate out the old cans. Dad was a much better prepper than I ever aspired to be. I only really got interested in his peculiar hobby the night before when aliens showed up and turned off the lights globally.

Charlene ordered her sons to shop at the rear of the store. It was pretty dark back there since the store's only light came through the big front windows. I said as much to Charlene, but she waved that away. "They'll make out. What's gotten into you, Mr. Rifleman?"

I shrugged. "That old bag taught me in school. After almost thirty-some years of her bullshit, I figured it was time I said something. Today's a day for telling it like it is and living our truth, right? If not now, when?"

"That's a lot of gumption for you, isn't it, Kent?" She didn't say it in a mean way. More like she was concerned for my mental well-being.

"Mrs. Greensby's been on my enemies list for a long time. If you've got something to say to somebody, it's good to get it off your chest before the aliens land, invade, and lay eggs in our corpses."

I was surprised by her look of approval. "Well, look at you! Still waters do indeed run deep."

Charlene's clot of boys scrambled back up the aisle, clearly excited to have the run of the place. I spotted several cereal boxes in their carts that weren't much more than candy. I had no doubt they wanted to get home and feast until they were sick. I wanted to do the same.

When I thought of all the things I didn't eat anymore, I wanted to steal a few of the Pino family's colorful cereals. When Mom was alive, she cut up my hotdogs and put a dab of ketchup on each one. Birthday candles for lunch, she'd called them. And when was the last time I ate a whole pizza without counting carbs? Or made a box of mac and cheese and ate the whole wad of cheesy glue straight out of the pot? I spotted a box of Oreos on a high shelf the Pino boys had missed and tossed it in my basket.

Charlene and the boys went up to the front counter. With Edna Greensby in his ear, he looked at the Pino family's three carts of groceries and shook his head. "We're closed, Missus."

"The hell you are," I said. "Write up her purchases."

"Can't purchase nothin'," Burt said. "Look around. No lights, no juice to the till."

"She said she'd give you an IOU," I said. "You're gonna settle for that, Burt. From where I stand, it's take her IOU or you get air pudding and walk away pie."

Edna Greensby laughed as the youngest Pino boy began to cry.

Burt kept shaking his head until I hefted the M41A to rest the butt of the stock on my hip. I gave him the look that said, *Well?*

"I've got a running tally," the oldest Pino boy said. "It comes to $312 dollars before taxes."

I didn't remember his name, but I knew he was the man of the house while his father worked up north in Alberta's oil fields. The kid had something I envied. With his mother's good looks and his father's tall, muscular frame, he had a confidence that I'd never possessed at eighteen or nineteen.

Hell, I thought. *I didn't start acting spineful and spiteful until the aliens showed up. Or maybe it's the rifle in my hands and the pistol in my belt.*

The weight of the rifle and the warmth of the pistol under my shirt in the small of my back gave me strength. I should have been embarrassed by that. In the movie scripts I'd written, I preferred heroes who fought with their fists. However, truth to tell, I liked the look of self-doubt that crossed Burt's face as I glared at him.

Edna Greensby was undeterred. "Don't you people understand English? Mr. Caldwell told you he's closed. You can't have any of this. Now go put it back on the shelves before I call the police."

"How you gonna call the police, Mrs. Greensby?" I asked. "Shout out the front door and hope Sheriff Sawatsky can hear you?"

"I came in here to get a few necessities," my old teacher said primly. "I didn't come here for your sass!"

"The sass is free. Go about your business and get your necessities. I'm sure if Burt will take your IOU, he'll give anybody the benefit of the doubt."

The old woman huffed and nearly tripped over Jordan's wagon as she hurried toward the far aisle. Once she was behind the shelves and out of sight, she shouted, "None of you deserve *anything!*"

A neuron that had been inactive for a long time fired up. I was reminded of a trip to Portland I took with my Dad. It was our first trip out of town since cancer took my mother. Dad wasn't big on shopping, but my sister was. We followed Catherine around the city, from boutique to shopping center and back. Catherine was a slow shopper, too.

As Dad and I stood around waiting, he pointed to a fancy store. "Son? You know what your sister sees when she's poking through all these stores?"

I answered without hesitation, "Her future."

"What do *you* see?"

"A lot of stuff we don't got."

He laughed hard at that. "Tha's right! A lot of stuff we don't got!"

"Whatever you've got budgeted for this trip to assuage our grief, I'm okay, Dad. Spend it all on Catherine. This is more her thing than mine."

I'm sure Dad must have hugged me at my mother's funeral, but I honestly don't remember. But I do remember that moment in Portland. Dad hugged me long and hard in public in the middle of a busy mall and didn't care who saw him do it.

When he finally stepped back, he said, "You deserve everything, Kent. I wish I could give you everything."

As Burt capitulated and wrote an IOU for Charlene to sign, an entirely new thought hit me: *I deserve better.*

While Burt double-checked the eldest Pino boy's math, Edna Greensby steamed up behind me. Her focus was on Jordan who now stood beside me. "This your father?"

"My uncle," she replied.

"Well, tell your mother you shouldn't spend any time with this man. He's bad."

Jordan fixed her with her bright blue eye. "He's bad? Bad? Really? That's all you got? Uncle Kent says you taught him and my mom. I hope it wasn't English. Your vocabulary sucks."

Shocked into silence, the old woman stood staring at us.

Jordan looked up at me and smiled. "Mom and Dad call you the slug-about. It's mean, but at least it's a little clever."

"Slug-about? That's kinda funny. I always thought your mother should marry an English nobleman from a couple centuries past. Instead, she married a plumber from Silverton. Saul's got a pretty good vocabulary, huh?"

My niece nodded sagely while we waited for the Pino family to clear the way. The littlest Pino boy had stopped crying. Charlene gave me a bright smile and mouthed a thank you.

Stepping up to the counter, I was feeling much better than I had earlier. Burt still looked sour. "You done, Kent?"

"Just thinkin' we should have an alien invasion once a month or so."

We're out of electricity, I thought, *but I do have power.*

"You all good, Burt?"

"I don't have a calculator that works, but that boy's math with a pencil seemed to check out on paper."

We put our groceries on the counter. Burt's slow math skills made me want to call the Pino boy back to help. As Burt counted up what I owed him, Edna Greensby found her voice. "What makes a person so mean he isn't a person anymore?"

"People like you turn good people mean," I said.

She grimaced. "I remember teaching you and your sister. What would your mother think of you now, bullying an old woman and brandishing a gun?"

As I turned to face my old teacher, Jordan rolled her eye. "Here we go!"

"I'll tell you what I remember," I said. "One sunny May morning after my first year away, I came back to town on a break from school. I made myself a job washing windows up and down Main Street. Burt there hired me, too. You came along and mocked me. You asked me if washing windows was the only job I could get after being away at college. I'd only been away for a few months. I don't know what you expected. Was I supposed to be trading stock options or curing cancer or something?"

"Don't be so touchy. What's the matter? Can't take a little teasing?"

"Why should I? Besides, you weren't teasing. You were trying to make me feel small. That's what small people do. You know, when I said your face was a wrinkly old mask hiding a monster, I wasn't joking. Can't blame age or dementia. You were always like this."

Emma Greensby left without her groceries. Burt waited until the door was closed behind her. Then he let out a chuckle. "What has gotten into you, man?"

I smiled. "Some people cruise their entire lives depending on others to be too polite. Past time somebody called her out on her stink."

Jordan looked up at me. "That was a good takedown of Mrs. Greensby. You practice that at home? Like, in front of the mirror?"

"Maybe so," I admitted. "I've been wanting to tell her off about that window washing shaming thing since the day happened."

"Jeez, you can hold a grudge!" Burt exclaimed.

"I've got a good memory."

As we stepped into the street, Jordan pointed to the eastern sky. "Still no jets and the alien ship has barely moved all the time we were in there. What do you think it means?"

"I don't know any more than you do, Cyclops."

She giggled. "Mom hates when you call me that."

"Oh? What do you have to say about that?"

"What you told me," she replied. "Bullshit is your love language. If I told you not to say it, you wouldn't. There are plenty of Jordans in the world, but I don't know anybody with the nickname of Cyclops. I'm special."

"You are my favorite niece," I said.

"I'm your only niece."

"So keep your stats up in case your mom and dad decide to introduce new competition into the mix. You better watch out and stay frosty. Babies are awfully cute."

"Hey!"

I turned away from the spaceship to find an even more interesting surprise. Kyle Rickles stood in the middle of the street. He held a deer rifle aimed at my head.

"Hello, again, Kyle. Julie send you home?"

"*Shut up, Schreiber!*"

"What's the deal, man? Aliens are hanging in the sky, and you suddenly lose your mind? I don't know where the sheriff is, do you?"

"Looks to me like this could be the end of the world," Kyle said. "I wanna get the respect I deserve, and you got no respect."

Uh-oh, I thought. *This new truth-telling thing cuts both ways.*

"I don't like how you talked to Julie, and I never liked the way you looked at her. This has been a long time coming, Schreiber."

"Has it? I hardly think about you at all."

Kyle advanced until he stood ten paces from me. He cast a mean glance Jordan's way. "Get out of the street and out of the way, kid. Your uncle's going to put his rifle down, get on his knees, and grovel. I demand an apology."

Jordan picked up a can of salmon from her wagon and threw it at him as hard as she could. My niece was the smartest and nicest person I knew. Unfortunately, her many good traits did not make up for her terrible depth perception. She missed our assailant by several feet.

"Don't do that again," Kyle said.

Jordan picked up a tin of tuna and hucked it at him. She was closer this time, but she still missed.

Kyle fired his rifle in the air. I should have shot him then, but I was distracted by my niece turning to grab me tight.

As she burrowed her nose into my sternum, Kyle laughed at us. "Who's hiding behind skirts now? Drop the rifle in the dirt, Kent. Tell your mouthy brat to take her little red wagon on home." Then he pointed his rifle at Jordan.

"Go on home, Cyclops. Kyle and I will have a civil conversation."

She stayed put until I dropped the rifle. As it clattered to the ground, Jordan peeled herself off me and pulled the pistol from the small of my back in one smooth motion. Her voice shaking, Jordan ordered Kyle to put his weapon down.

He grinned at her. "You're just a little girl. I've got a big gun, and you've got a little pistol. You also have a history of missing. I wonder why."

"You've got a deer rifle and can only take one shot before you have to rack another cartridge. I can keep squeezing this trigger until the mag is empty. I figure I'll home in on your belly before it clicks empty."

Impressed, I let out a low whistle. "Cyclops has a point. I wonder how many rounds she'll put in you after you take one shot at me? There are no cars so there's no ambulance. No ambulance means no help from Salem Hospital."

Kyle turned his rifle on Jordan, and I stepped in front of her. She peered around me, her gun hand still aiming in his general direction.

"Eyes on me," I told him. "I want you to think about this. Folks around here have mixed feelings about me, but if you shoot that weapon anywhere near a child, how much do you think your life will be worth? A nickel? Less? And you'll never get Julie back. She babysat Jordan when she was a baby. You think you'll ever get her back if you even think about pulling that trigger? Do you even have to think about it?"

"I hate you, Kent."

"Sure you do, but that's not the issue."

"What's the issue?"

"My niece is holding a pistol. Her aim may be questionable, but she's got enough shots to zero in on your wide ass. You're sweaty and your hands are shaking now. Not for nothin', her gun hand is steady as a rock."

That wasn't true, but I was riffing off a line from one of my film scripts and it sounded good. At least, it sounded good enough. Kyle Rickles lowered his rifle.

In that moment, shielding my niece and yet protected by her, I was so proud. Proud of her and proud of me. Maybe for the first time since Dad had hugged me in that mall years before, I felt like I was enough.

I borrowed a line from the social influencer on TikTok, "This is America. We can be better than this."

I think Kyle was about to curse me out and walk away. There's a danger in trying to get the last word in an argument. Hang in there too long to have your say and you might finally get clobbered. I did not hear the explosion. What I remember is the odd sensation of seeing the mid-afternoon sunlight overpowered. I didn't understand what was happening at first. All I knew was a blinding white light enveloped everything. It was as if the town of Knock Station were suddenly bleached white by a searing force.

Jordan and I were facing west, away from the alien craft. Kyle got the brunt of that first blast. He screeched and collapsed to the street, covering his eyes, but too late. For Kyle Rickles, the term blinding light was not merely an expression.

Disoriented, Jordan and I clung to each other. I threw her to the ground and covered her body with mine as the heat hit us. The sound of the explosion arrived, shaking the ground. The explosion seemed to go on and on. I worried it would never stop.

Jordan yelled something in my ear, but amid the din of destruction, I couldn't make out her words. A hot wind whipped over us. Her little wagon flew down the street as if it had been kicked by an invisible giant.

Slowly, the hot maelstrom eased its fury. I don't know how long we lay in the street. I remember the screaming. Some of that noise came from Kyle Rickles. Some of it came from Jordan. A little of that yelling probably came from me.

The pain at the nape of my neck and down the backs of my bare forearms felt like a stinging hot slap that wouldn't stop. I'd been stung by a wasp once. It felt a lot like that. My ears rang. My jangled nerves felt like I'd been injected with venom.

Stunned, I managed to get up on unsteady legs. To my overwhelmed senses, the street swung and rolled beneath my feet as if I stood on the deck of a small boat in a terrible storm.

I was afraid to look, but curiosity made me turn to look to the east and skyward. A mushroom cloud reached from the horizon to high in the sky. Out of the massive black cloud, the alien ship emerged. On fire and leaking plumes of grey smoke, the craft fell to Earth in slow motion.

Jordan pulled on my sleeve, but I had a hard time hearing over the high whine in my ears. She ran off after the wagon, and I staggered after her in a daze. I vaguely remember walking around Kyle. The skin on his face and hands was as red as a boiled lobster. He said something to me, but I was too out of it to understand his words.

My niece was on her knees beside the wagon. It lay on its side, its wheels still turning in the hot wind. She wept as she gathered what she could of our groceries.

Stiffly, painfully, I bent to help her. The cans of soup were warm from the explosion's wash. Too rattled, I dropped on my ass to rest. Looking around, I discovered every window had been shattered.

The ringing in my ears didn't go away, but it receded enough that I could hear Jordan crying.

"Hey," I called weakly. "C'mere, Cyclops."

She knelt beside me, then dropped into my lap. I held her like I had when she was a baby, cradling her head in the crook of my elbow.

My arms and neck and the backs of my ears still hurt where the fierce light had burned me. However, I smiled as I stared down into her ice-blue eye. "Thanks for coming to my rescue. You're my hero, Jordan."

"I was scared," she said. "I thought I couldn't be more frightened, but I am now. What happened?"

I looked to the east again. The alien ship had dropped out of sight but the mushroom cloud remained. "The government nuked the aliens."

"Next to us?"

"Not next to us. Perspective is hard. The ship must have been even bigger than we thought. If it were really close, we would have been vaporized. We must be at the edge of the blast radius. I remember pictures of old nuclear tests. Naval ships would get close enough to watch the show. We got the show, alright."

"Too close!"

"Better here than over a more populated area, I suppose ... from their perspective, I mean. For us, it sucks. I bet there isn't a tree or a house still standing for miles over that way. The landscape must have spared us some of the shockwave."

"What do we do, Uncle Kent?"

"About what?"

"Getting radiation poisoning! When I closed my eyes, it was still bright. You were on top of me, and I swear I could see through you. I saw your skeleton!"

"How'd I look?"

"Not good."

"I forgot to smile for my X-ray."

"Don't joke! What do we do?"

Still in a daze, I scanned the street. Burt came out of the grocery store holding a bloody rag to his head. Kyle was still rolling around on the ground. I didn't see Edna Greensby anywhere, but I didn't miss her.

"If we were any closer, we'd have died instantly," I said absently.

Jordan dried the tears from her eye. "So we're going to be okay?"

No, I thought.

"Yes," I said.

Still cradling her like a baby, I reached out, plucked a small box from the ground, and tore away the plastic with my teeth. "Oreo? I want the whole box."

And painkillers, I thought. *I need a lot of painkillers.*

The cookies were so warm that the white filling was soft and melting. For a few minutes, I didn't dwell on the past or the future. I focused on the sweetness of the cookies and the sweetness of the moment. It was the only power I had left, and I was determined to use it.

The forest was on fire, and our cars didn't work so there was no escape. Radiation sickness would soon set in. I wasn't sure which would kill us first, but in one short trip to the grocery store, I'd redefined who I was. The joke was that none of it mattered. No one would be around to eulogize me. There'd be no snarky remarks at my funeral. No one would have the last word.

I am Kent Schreiber of Knock Station, I thought. *Right now, I am enough. As soon as I try to stand up and walk into the future, I will find it is both terrible and short. I will eat this entire bag of Oreos with my little niece. This is our last good time. I will make it last.*

This is the way it is.

VII

War is a sprint.
Survival is a marathon.

HUMANS IN NATURE

Major Melamed sat before a bank of monitors ninety feet below Little Rock Air Force Base. Dumbfounded, he listened to the report from Colorado. "A frigate? Really?"

"Yes, sir! What do you suppose the point of that was? Over."

A demonstration of power to intimidate us and force our hand, Melamed thought. However, he did not answer the question. *As soon as I'm done talking to Colorado, I'm going to get drunk.*

Only one screen still functioned. The monitor showed the alien prisoner AKA Cinnamon. Radio signals faded in and out, but before they left, the communications techs figured a way to open a line to NORAD. There was no video feed. The scratchy audio was weak and unstable.

Staring at the alien on his screen, Melamed realized he hadn't listened to the last transmission from NORAD. "Colorado? Repeat your last message. Over."

"Good news, sir. Baltimore, Los Angeles, Austin, and Helsinki are not down! Those reports are confirmed false. I repeat, false! Just trolls messing up our intel! And it looks like the nukes took down every alien craft! They're all down! I repeat, all Tangos down! Over!"

"But the radiation, what's the Curie measure? How many nukes fired? What's the rad count? Over."

"We don't have that information yet, sir. Over."

I've been picturing the fall of civilization all wrong, the major thought. *The end of the world will happen, but it won't be explained or be televised.*

"There is more, sir! My sister's in Baltimore! There's a chance she got through this. With the grid down, there's still a lot of people who don't know about the invasion at all. My sister is probably still sitting at home, oblivious. This is a great victory! We're all celebrating here! Every move we made in defense of the planet will be second-guessed by any amateur experts who survived. Conspiracy theorists and every UFO nut will never shut up, but we did it! We defeated the aliens!"

Melamed hadn't realized he'd been holding his breath until he let it out in a long sigh. "Yes ... very good news, sure." He shook his head as he acknowledged the transmission.

NORAD's Intel officer was so upbeat, the major tamped down the urge to burst his bubble. His contact sounded young and not very bright. Even if all the alien craft were destroyed, the best-case scenario was grim.

Radiation burns, sickness, and famine would lead to mass death and mass migration. Economies would collapse. What supplies might remain would be hoarded.

"Sir? Are you still there? Come back, Little Rock! Over!"

Melamed keyed his mic. "My fear, Colorado, is today we have achieved a Pyrrhic victory."

"Sir? I know the environmental impacts are grave, but we have experts here who point to Fukushima and Hiroshima. They managed that nuclear power plant meltdown and flowers grow in Hiroshima. Our people say we're going to get through this."

Easy for you to say, Melamed thought. *You're hiding in a hardened site with a lifetime supply of Twinkies and iodine pills. And how many of your experts agree we can shake this off in a decade or less?* "What else have you got, Colorado?"

"Scattered reports, but we are sure every known alien craft is down, sir. When we targeted them, most were in rural areas. The most kinetic areas were far north. We minimized civilian casualties. Glass jaws to our atomic punch! Looks like they didn't know so much about us after all!" the Comms officer crowed.

Melamed wondered idly if Iceland, or some warm tropical country far to the south might be spared. *If I could find a pilot, maybe … no.*

He'd missed his chance to flee.

The major keyed his microphone again. "Roger that, Colorado. My congratulations to your superiors on the counterattack. Any news on Colonel Hannah Fresco? She was ordered to report to the Ark. She had a medical team and a couple of alien corpses with her."

After a long pause, the Intelligence officer came back. "She's on my list, but she's not checked in. Same with any of the medical team. I'm sorry, but if we had alien corpses under the mountain, I'm sure I would have heard about that. Over."

"So what are you saying, son?"

"The big doors are closed, sir. I'm sorry to report that it's very likely Colonel Fresco's on the nasty side of those doors."

Fresco's out there somewhere, Melamed thought, *either dead or marooned on the ground.*

Mechanics had managed to get her C-130 off the tarmac, but Melamed guessed her plane had gone down, probably due to friendly fire. The last known positions of the alien ships dotted the northern hemisphere. Nukes had taken the invaders down, but navigating the flight path from Arkansas to Colorado had been a gamble. Melamed understood the allure of getting to NORAD's doomsday ark, but combatting the ripples of the pressure waves alone would be a nightmare for any pilot. The major found himself grateful he'd been tasked with staying with the prisoner.

The major asked if the brass had any orders for him.

"It's a little crazy here right now, sir. I don't have any orders to pass on."

"Standing by for further orders. Tango Mike, Colorado. Over and out."

The Intel officer in Colorado wished him luck. The major could detect no hint of irony in the young man's tone. He was stuck in the vault with Cinnamon. Melamed had a few boxes of MREs and the slim hope that NORAD would expend the fuel to rescue him before his supplies ran out.

Only two guards remained on the base. When Colonel Fresco left with the other guards and the medical team, the pair of guards waved goodbye. The men had volunteered to stay behind, and both were asleep in their racks. When they'd helped capture the alien, they'd acted nearly euphoric, high on adrenaline. As the hours crept by, both men turned somber and complained of exhaustion. The major suspected depression was already setting in. He would let the men have their much-needed rest and fill them in on his communication with NORAD when they woke.

They know what we're facing next, he thought. *War is a sprint. Survival is a marathon.*

Within twenty-four hours of the EMP blast, techs figured out how to get some trucks rolling and several planes back in the air. The base commander ordered most personnel to bug out. There hadn't been enough transport for everyone to go where they wanted. Some left for home. Others swore that since most of the alien ships were in the northern hemisphere, the smart move was to head south. Others simply headed into Jacksonville to get drunk.

Melamed felt as lonely as if he were marooned on a tiny desert island. The major wished the Vault wasn't so much like a tomb. The gray walls needed color and he needed sunlight. He wondered when he'd see the sun again.

Earth's counterattack had been successful, but he had no one to tell except his prisoner. Melamed's gaze fell on the screen that monitored the alien. Cinnamon stood in his cage, as motionless as a statue. The alien's stillness was uncanny. Sometimes the major wondered if they were dealing with a machine made to look like a monster. The tentacles around the red slash of a mouth and the white bulbous head would rival any horror dreamed up by a Hollywood props department.

Melamed checked his sidearm's load and made his way down to the Vault's detention area. In deference to the alien's wishes and in an attempt to establish a rapport, the major had dimmed the lights. Striding into the room, he flipped the spotlights to full power again.

"Wake up, Cinnamon! I'm annoyed with you. Your people — excuse me, your *kind* — dropped a frigate in the interior of California! You murdered a bunch of innocent people in Central Park!"

Tall, hideous, and unreadable, the alien turned its head a few inches to regard him. "But you have news of your victory, yes?"

Melamed broke his stride, his confidence dented. "You know that thing where you can talk to me with your translator? Were you in contact with your fleet, too?"

"No. Your species is simply predictable. I did warn you of that."

Melamed covered his rising anger and, with feigned casualness, sat in a chair opposite the alien. "Here's the bad news for you, Cinnamon. Your fleet is destroyed."

"That is interesting. I did not expect to live to hear of it."

"You thought we'd kill you or maybe vivisect you?"

"The fact that I am alive is a statistical anomaly, what you would call a one in a million chance."

"You didn't think humans could destroy your fleet."

"I believe you thought that," Cinnamon replied.

"Nonetheless, here we are, winner and loser."

"That is true," the alien agreed.

Melamed leaned forward in his seat. "We are so different. I don't suppose it is possible we could have enough in common to understand each other?"

The alien tilted its enormous head. "We understand you very well. Our species are not so different."

"My people value life."

"Yet you come here in triumph to announce that my ships are destroyed."

"I value *human* life, anyway. You lost the right to my sympathy when your species attacked mine."

"Did we really do so much to provoke you? How many of your species have you sacrificed to repel mine?"

Melamed rose from his chair. He carried a Beretta M9 on his hip, and he wanted to empty all fifteen rounds into Cinnamon. Jaw clenched in agitation, he paced back and forth.

"You have not won, Major Melamed. I told you precisely what would happen, and it has, hasn't it?"

"You're thinking of the nuclear radiation. I know! I have the same concerns. But the point is, we can rebuild. Someone once said the two most powerful words in the English language are *begin again* — "

"And begin again is what we will do, Major. Thank you."

"Thank me? What are you talking about?"

"Your planet is on fire."

"Your ships are down! Our forests are burning, but all of *you* are dead. You're the last, the sole survivor, and probably not for much longer. Or maybe we should put you in a museum. We have a struggle ahead, though. We probably won't have time for museums and memorials for a decade or two."

"Your planet is about to become my planet. I believe the common phrase is: thank you for your service."

Melamed drew his weapon from its holster. "I could ask you about your technology, your culture, and your beliefs. All that would be very interesting to somebody, but given what you made us do, I don't care. You lose." He raised the M9.

"The Arctic is on fire, is it not? Forests across the northern hemisphere are spewing smoke, correct?"

The major wiped sweat from his eyes and took careful aim at the alien's huge head.

"Methane is being released from the tundra. Fires across the planet are turning the skies black. Climate change has now accelerated by many years. We provided the targets, and you provided the means to effect the change we required. This is not the first time you have been drawn into a war that ultimately did more damage to you than to your enemies. I thank you, because my mission is complete.

We could not have accomplished so much without your cooperation."

Melamed lowered his weapon and stepped closer to peer into the alien's giant yellow eyes. "You're lying! You've lost everything. Your ships are obliterated! The crews are all dead!"

"I omitted information, but I did not lie." The alien reached out, its nine-fingered hand spread against the inside of his prison's screen. Melamed's stomach turned when he saw the suckers that lined the too-long fingers of each hand. The screen cracked, then shattered. The alien stepped through. Thick glass crunched under the alien's great weight.

My God, they were right! These things do smell like cinnamon!

"First, we sent a pair of small scout ships. We arrived on your planet in the 1940s. We watched your wars and marked your patterns."

"So?"

"The Mortchallin are patient. That was merely an expeditionary force to reconnoiter, to observe your actions and reactions. I myself helped to confirm the observations made by the scouts. Your planet is ripe for geoengineering."

The alien did not make a move toward him, but Melamed kept his weapon trained on Cinnamon's head. "Tell me why I shouldn't kill you right now?"

"Yes, why don't you? I am a statistical anomaly. They do happen and I am prepared to die, Major. I was meant to perish in your nuclear firestorm."

"What are you saying? Speak plain. What's the plan?"

"The plan has been executed. A Mortchallin generation ship is on its way. In seven to ten of your years, a new population will become inhabitors of your planet. Whatever's left of humans will serve us well."

"You intend to make us slaves?"

"I told you before. Survivors will be bred and farmed."

"Like cattle?" Melamed shouted. "We don't deserve this."

"Our conflict was never based on what anyone deserved, Major.

To survive, the Mortchallin must dominate. We have colonized many planets. Our biology is such that we produce many progeny, and we live much longer than humans do. That is one of the things I admire about your species. You live such short lives and so many of you suffer illness. You are fragile and die easily. Your biology ensures that you will make room for your descendants. That is what I am doing. My life's end and that of those scouts who came with me will provide a home for generations of my kind. I was born for sacrifice."

Melamed cursed as he wiped sweat from his eyes with his free hand again. His heart pounded so hard, it felt as if the organ were trying to escape his ribcage. His hand shaking, he managed to keep the M9 trained on the prisoner. "I've never hated anything more than I hate you, Cinnamon."

"An understandable response. I can offer you one consolation, Major. Because the last remaining humans will be farmed, we will not allow your species to become extinct."

"We're not cattle! We're sentient beings!" Melamed spat.

"Are you really so sentient? I warned what was coming and it still happened. You have a history of not heeding warnings. That was a major variable in our calculations."

The alien sank to the floor suddenly, panting. "I can still function, but the mix of gases in your atmosphere is suboptimal. I tire easily. From my observations, it's highly probable you will use your weapon in the next few seconds. Aim for the head. It is where I am most vulnerable."

Melamed lowered his weapon. "Maybe the answer is improbable. You are my enemy, a spy for an invading force. Your species has committed genocide. The Mortchallin intend to enslave any human survivors, if there are any left by the time that ship arrives."

"And?"

"What if I proved you wrong? I asked you your real name before, and you wouldn't tell me. Let's start there."

"To what end, Major?"

"The war's over. What if I changed the variables and did the unexpected?" Melamed placed his pistol on the concrete floor. "Let's discuss alternatives. Let's do what we should have tried in the first place. I propose opening diplomatic relations. With your technology, you could be more than conquerors. You asked me what my name meant — "

"Strong teacher. I remember."

"This is your opportunity to be more than murderers ranging across the galaxy taking planet after planet. Teach us. By the time the rest of your race arrives, maybe we could change. If we can get past our anger, we could learn so much from each other. How about it?"

On impulse, Melamed stepped close enough to touch the alien. "You say you're a scientist. You've researched us for decades. You must be curious. Curiosity is the root of all intelligence, isn't it?"

When the alien made no move, the major reached out slowly with his right hand. "You've seen us shake hands, right? It's a gesture of goodwill. When two parties of equal stature meet, it's how we signal that we are friendly."

Slowly, the alien extended one of its arms. The nine-fingered hand closed on Melamed's hand, cool and smooth, big enough to swallow his hand and wrap up his forearm.

"My true name, known only to those in my family, is — " The alien made a noise no human vocal cords could replicate.

"And I am Boaz. Nice to meet you. Shall we begin negotiations? We are better than you think. Or we could be."

"You're not as good as you think you are." The alien's hand closed tighter around the major's hand and arm, driving him to his knees in pain.

Melamed gasped. "You have superior technology! You crossed the galaxy! You must be better than soulless, merciless conquerors."

But superiority in one area didn't translate to possessing a moral compass. When the alien pressed down, squeezing tight, the major had his answer. Before pain overwhelmed his senses, Melamed's last thought was, *This is the way it's going to be.*

The last thing the major saw was the red slash of the alien's drooling maw open wide. Its tentacles shot out to grab his head. Long suckers sealed the major's mouth and nose. One of the tentacles rammed down his throat. Major Boaz Melamed couldn't even scream as the alien pulled him into three rows of razor-sharp teeth.

When the alien's feast was done, the monster bent over what remained of the body. "We are not better than this. We are merely better than you. *Kintela Chumagen.*

The End of the Beginning.

THANK YOU FOR READING

If you dig *Our Alien Hours*, please leave a review.

You'll find detailed lists of my books on the following pages.

To keep up to date on new releases, deals, and news, please sign up for my newsletter at AllThatChazz.com to join the Inner Circle.

DYSTOPIAN & APOCALYPTIC BOOKS BY ROBERT CHAZZ CHUTE

This Plague of Days

What will you do to protect your family in the zombie apocalypse? Young Jaimie Spencer is an unlikely hero amid the ashes and ruins of our world. On the spectrum and selectively mute, he's more obsessed with his dictionary than with the fate of humanity. However, before this epic story is over, Good will do battle with Evil and Jaimie is our champion.

Robert's most successful series to date, *This Plague of Days* won Honorable Mention in their Self-published Ebook Awards from *Writers' Digest*. All three seasons of this trilogy are available as an omnibus or individually as ebooks and paperbacks.

Endemic

She was a nail. She is a hammer.

As the United States falls to disease, killers and thieves rule New

York. Bookish, neurotic, and nerdy, Ovid Fairweather finds herself trapped in the struggle for survival.

Bullied by her father, haunted by her dead therapist, and hunted by marauders, Ovid is forced to fight. With only the voices in her head as her guides, an unlikely heroine will become a queen.

∽

AFTER Life

Zombies will soon invade the United States. Which side will you join, the infected or the damned?

Artificial Facilitation Therapy for Enhanced Response (AFTER) was a biomimetic stem cell nanotechnology with numerous health and wellness applications. Then a military contractor weaponized it using brain parasites. When the zombie apocalypse arrives, we soon discover that genetically engineered zombies are hard to kill.

Officer Daniel Harmon is tasked with stopping the epidemic. Dr. Chloe Robinson needs to get her creation back under control. We can't always get what we want.

The *AFTER Life* trilogy is available in ebook and in paperback.

∽

Citizen Second Class

Set a decade later in the same universe as *Endemic*, Kismet is a young woman who must travel to Atlanta to find work to feed what's left of her family. The city has become a fortress for rich religious zealots who care nothing for the poor. Just below the surface, a revolution simmers as disaster looms. Join the fight.

~

Amid Mortal Words

A dangerous stranger met on a train leaves behind a powerful book. With mere words, this book could destroy the world or save it. This power is now in the hands of one man relying on a mysterious woman to guide him toward the Apocalypse or away from our destruction. It's a roller coaster ride filled with twists and turns toward a surprising conclusion that will keep you up all night reading.

~

Robot Planet

The robots are unfailingly polite until the moment they kill you. This future isn't merely a forbidding dystopia. It's cyberpunk scary. In this series of four novellas, three very different people join forces to combat the rise of the Next Intelligence. The odds are against us.
Start your next adventure by grabbing *Robot Planet, The Complete Series*, available in paperback or ebook.

~

Haunting Lessons (with Holly Pop)

This is not a ghost story. It only starts out that way. Tamara Smith is a young woman from the Midwest who experiences an unspeakable tragedy. Soon she sees apparitions. That's only the beginning of her adventures. Running away to New York, she soon discovers a secret world of dark magic doing combat with alien forces from another dimension.

If she is to save the world from the coming invasion, Tam must train to become a leader among the Choir Invisible. She fights for us all.

Death Lessons, Fierce Lessons, and *Dream's Dark Flight* are also part of this series of gripping adventures.

～

All Empires Fall

How will the world end? In this short story collection, Robert shares several tales of the apocalypse. It comes in flood and fire. It stabs at us out of the darkness of space.

Robert Chazz Chute many dark ideas for you to consider and revel in as you stay up through the night, turning pages to each ending of our world.

～

Our Zombie Hours (First in the *Apocalyptic Tales Series*)

Strap in for five adventures from the front line of the zombie apocalypse. As society collapses, humans often prove themselves more dangerous than the infected. Enjoy these fresh stories that explore survival, heroism, and betrayal in a world gone mad. A fun night of horror awaits.

ALL BOOKS BY ROBERT CHAZZ CHUTE

~ DYSTOPIAN AND APOCALYPTIC FICTION ~

This Plague of Days, Season 1
This Plague of Days, Season 2
This Plague of Days, Season 3
This Plague of Days, Omnibus Edition

THE AFTER Life TRILOGY
Inferno
Purgatory
Paradise
AFTER Life (Box Set)

Endemic
Citizen Second Class

Amid Mortal Words

Robot Planet, The Complete Series

The Dimension War Series:
Haunting Lessons
Death Lessons
Fierce Lessons
Dream's Dark Flight

~ TIME TRAVEL ~

Wallflower

~ CRIME THRILLERS ~

The Night Man

Brooklyn in the Mean Time

The Hit Man Series:
Bigger Than Jesus
Higher Than Jesus
Hollywood Jesus
Resurrection

~ COLLECTIONS ~

Murders Among Dead Trees
Sometime Soon, Somewhere Close
Self-help for Stoners
All Empires Fall
Our Zombie Hours
Our Alien Hours

~ NONFICTION ~

Do the Thing: The Last Stress-busting Book You'll Ever Need

Find links to all my books
AllThatChazz.com

ACKNOWLEDGMENTS

Gari Strawn of strawnediting.com always has my back. Thank you, Editrix Supreme!

Many thanks also to Russ Sawatsky for his excellent contributions in beta reading.

ABOUT THE AUTHOR

Robert Chazz Chute is a former crime and science journalist. A winner of eight writing awards, he pens fiction full-time from Other London.

For updates, links to his books, and Patreon support of his fiction podcasts, please visit Robert at AllThatChazz.com.